"In Case You've Forgotten, And I'm Sure You Have, My High School Reunion Is Tonight."

"I know that," Raleigh said. "Rebecca, I'm sorry—"

"I know, I know. You won't be able to be my date. Well, we both knew even before our talk that you would have come up with a last-minute excuse not to go with me."

He opened his mouth to speak, but she cut him off.

"You're off the hook. That's right. You don't have to suffer the embarrassment of being caught with Reb Barnett. Sure, a few people know we've been seeing each other, but don't worry. There's no proof that the girl from the wrong side of the river ever got close to you. No one's ever claimed that, anyway. And if someone had, who would believe it?" She slammed the door in his face.

Don't miss the romantic adventures of the other GIRLS MOST LIKELY TO... coming your way in 1997—only in Silhouette Desire!

Dear Reader,

Happy holidays from the staff at Silhouette Desire! As you can see by the special cover treatment this month, these books are our holiday gifts to you. And each and every story is so wonderful that I know you'll want to buy extras to give to your friends!

We begin with Jackie Merritt's MAN OF THE MONTH, *Montana Christmas*, which is the conclusion of her spectacular MADE IN MONTANA series. The fun continues with *Instant Dad*, the final installment in Raye Morgan's popular series THE BABY SHOWER.

Suzannah Davis's *Gabriel's Bride* is a classic— and sensuous—love story you're sure to love. And Anne Eames's delightful writing style is highlighted to perfection in *Christmas Elopement*. For a story that will make you feel all the warmth and goodwill of the holiday season, don't miss Kate Little's *Jingle Bell Baby*.

And Susan Connell begins a new miniseries— THE GIRLS MOST LIKELY TO... —about three former high school friends who are now all grown up in *Rebel's Spirit*. Look for upcoming books in the series in 1997.

Happy holidays and happy reading from

Lucia Macro

AND THE STAFF OF SILHOUETTE DESIRE

Please address questions and book requests to:
Silhouette Reader Service
U.S.: 3010 Walden Ave., P.O. Box 1325, Buffalo, NY 14269
Canadian: P.O. Box 609, Fort Erie, Ont. L2A 5X3

SUSAN CONNELL
REBEL'S SPIRIT

SILHOUETTE *Desire*®
Published by Silhouette Books
America's Publisher of Contemporary Romance

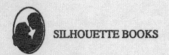

SILHOUETTE BOOKS

ISBN 0-373-76044-2

REBEL'S SPIRIT

Copyright © 1996 by Susan Connell

Printed in U.S.A.

Books by Susan Connell

Silhouette Desire

Reese: The Untamed #981
*Rebel's Spirit #1044

*The Girls Most Likely To...

SUSAN CONNELL

has a love of traveling that has taken her all over the world—Greece, Spain, Portugal, Central and South America, to name just a few places. While working for the foreign service she met a U.S. navy pilot, and eight days later they were engaged. Twenty-one years and several moves later, Susan, her husband, Jim, and daughter, Catherine, call the New Jersey shore home. When she's not writing, her part-time job at a local bookstore, Mediterranean cooking and traveling with her family are some of her favorite activities. Susan has been honored by New Jersey Romance Writers with their coveted Golden Leaf Award. She loves hearing from her readers.

For Cathy Connell
Thank heaven for little girls, they grow up in the most
delightful way...and with the best ideas!
Love, Mom

One

The thrill was back and building in the pit of Rebecca Barnett's stomach. Maybe the mixing scents of evergreen and chlorinated water had something to do with it, but she hadn't experienced such heady temptation since high school.

Stepping onto the diving board, she began lowering her towel, then stopped. A chilly breeze against her backside had her gasping with surprise. Was she crazy? She would have sworn she'd put this kind of bad-girl mischief behind her. A twenty-eight-year-old, self-made, successful businesswoman did not engage in these sorts of high jinks.

Clutching her towel closer, she looked down at the shimmering rectangle of bright blue water. Invitation pulsated in every drop. As a tingle of excitement began curling through her body, she felt her shoulders relaxing.

So what if the main reason she'd returned to Follett River was to impress everyone at her high school's ten-year reunion? That event wouldn't be taking place for another four weeks. Meanwhile, how often did a girl stumble on an opportunity like this?

Rising up on her toes she strained for a look outside the privacy fence. There was no one in sight.

No one to catch her in the act.

No one would ever know.

She lowered her heels to the roughened surface and bit back a smile.

"Except m-me," she said as another shiver began shaking her five-foot, eight-inch frame.

True, the unadulterated thrill of a stolen skinny-dip should not be reason enough to brave blustery November temperatures...but it was. And she knew why. This wasn't just anyone's swimming pool. Fate had made her the temporary tenant of Show-No-Mercy Hanlon, the nemesis of her senior year.

His Clark Kent appearance notwithstanding, one censoring look from those riveting hazel eyes and Mr. Hanlon had had her trembling with fears she couldn't even name. She still had to wonder why half the girls in Follett River High had managed to have major crushes on *him*—the history teacher from *Hades*. She shook her head. Some things, she guessed, were destined to remain a mystery to her.

Who cared? she thought, raking her fingers through her short, dark hair. She'd just found out that Show-No-Mercy Hanlon, now a professor at the local college, would be out of town until the end of the week. A smug smile of satisfaction was already tugging at her shivering lips. It had taken ten years and a twist of fate, but she was finally going to pull one over on him.

Loosening her towel, she twirled the bright red terry cloth above her head then pitched it over her shoulder. As goose bumps covered her body she could almost hear the raving voices of her old friends.

"Are you crazy, Reb? If Hanlon catches us, we'll be stuck in detention so long they'll be putting brass name plates on our chairs!"

Yes, this idea was most likely crazy. Certainly juvenile. But with Christmas just around the corner, even Santa's reindeer couldn't have dragged her off this diving board. "This one's for you, Hanlon!"

Running forward, she kicked up into the chilly autumn air then let loose a bloodcurdling whoop as she cannonballed into the pool. Steeling herself against the numbing cold, she began pulling herself through the water. Only sheer willpower kept her below the surface. The trip to the shallow end was upstream all the way, but that was no surprise. Wasn't everything in her life?

Raleigh Hanlon heard the shout and splash as he stepped out of his car in the driveway. Prayers and curses shared equal time under his breath as he sprinted for the gate. The old nightmare slamming against his heart was real again. *"Hold on!"* Why in hell had he put off closing the pool for so long? He riffled through his key ring, dropping it once before he located the right key. *"Please, hold on. Dammit, don't die!"*

Jamming the key into the lock, he gave it a hard twist, then kicked open the six-foot wall of wood. As he began struggling out of his jacket he saw the red towel lying behind the diving board and then the dark-haired form in the water. *"I'll get you out. Just take my hand, Buddy. Buddy, take my hand!"*

Raleigh's frantic movements stopped abruptly when a head, then shoulders surfaced at the shallow end. His heart was still hammering against his rib cage as he slumped against the fence. The whole business was a prank. A thoughtless, irresponsible prank. Anger welled where seconds before sheer terror had ruled. He was getting too damn old for this.

Pushing off the fence, he opened his mouth to speak. A split second later the intruder stood, stark naked and facing away from him. Raleigh slowly closed his mouth. His need to chastise vanished as he took in the sight before him. The incident might have "high school prank" written all over it, but *she* certainly didn't.

The slim brunette's womanly form glistened as if it were a live pink statue. Liquid light sparkled at her shoulders, played near the indentation of her spine and reflected off the pleasantly defined muscles in her back. His gaze dropped to where gentle wavelets were splashing against her firm bottom. The sight almost made up for the unfortunate placement of the pool which had her at the far end and facing away from him.

As he kept his gaze fixed to her backside he felt an undeniable tug of pure male awareness. Or was it recognition? Did he know her? He dragged his hand along his jaw as the need to call out to have her explain her presence slipped farther back in his mind.

When she pressed her thumbs against the sleek curves of her hips, all his righteous questions began disappearing from his head. Who cared how she'd gotten into the locked pool area? Who cared why she'd chosen *his* pool? Whoever she was, she was alive and presenting an admirable case for voyeurism. Dripping with a dangerous mixture of innocence and eroticism, she made every fantasy he'd ever had pale next to her reality.

As another revelation hit him, he shook his head. He'd spent his adult life teaching history, and only this moment did he finally understand how men could fight great wars over beauty such as this.

Right now he was waging war within himself. Should he continue to stare, or was it time to speak up? A smile pulled at his mouth when she laughed out loud then smacked the surface.

As he considered his dilemma further she let out an impassioned "Gotcha!" then leaned back into the water.

His heart thumped as he caught a glimpse of tightened pink nipples, an expanse of smooth, pale flesh and a neat triangle of dark hair at the apex of her thighs. Then water ribboned over her, distorting her perfection to a surreal dreamscape where fantasies melted and only heroic efforts could retrieve them.

He shoved an uneasy hand through his hair as memories of Buddy rushed in. He was no hero, he reminded himself. Hell, he couldn't even keep a naked woman out of his pool.

Impatience over the battling images got the better of him; he didn't suffer fools lightly, especially himself. His gaze circled the pool area, then landed back on the form moving through the water. He might be waking up in a hot sweat at three in the morning over this vision, but she'd be gone by then. Sent on her way with a stern warning he was already composing in his mind.

Judging the finishing point of her underwater swim, he walked down the landscaped steps to it and waited at the end of the pool until she came to him.

One last, languid stroke brought her to the surface. And there it was again. Even with her eyes shut and water streaming over her face and hair, he had an even stronger feeling that he knew her. Before he could place her, she was reaching up then closing her fingers over the top of his shoe. Her gracefully athletic move to haul herself out ended abruptly as she twisted her head to look up at him.

"You!" she said, releasing her grip. Sputtering, she dropped below the surface. A second later she came up clutching for the pool edge and shoving wet hair from her eyes. Eyes he'd seen before. Eyes filled with fear...or was that indignation? He cocked his head as a flash-back jolted through his consciousness.

Struggling to catch her breath, she locked gazes with him. "You're not supposed to be back until the week-end. W-what are you doing here?"

Indignation. Definitely indignation. "What am I do-ing here? This is my property. The question is, what are you doing here?"

Her mascara had smudged below her eyes, making them somehow bluer and wider and more vulnerable than he was sure she would want them to appear. She blinked, and the water beading on her lashes plopped onto her cheekbones.

"I've moved into Alan's apartment." Her gaze never left his as she pointed toward the garage.

"He never mentioned subletting. When did you talk to him about moving in?"

"I didn't. I talked to his sister. Megan said Alan would be away for the next six weeks and that you probably wouldn't mind if I took the place for, uh... " She stopped to lick a drop of water from her lips.

He felt his stern expression dissolving as his gaze riv-eted to where she was pressing her tongue. The tip glis-tened warm and pink in the late-afternoon light before she drew it slowly into her mouth again. The guileless gesture caught him off guard, causing a distinct stirring in the region of his groin. Her bare shoulders, high cheekbones and slicked-back hair, against that background of blue water, reminded him of a travel poster he'd seen for Tahiti. But this was November in New Jersey. Instead of orchids, the water around his lovely, but foolhardy, intruder was decorated with ripples from the wind. None of that mattered; she was easily the most exotic creature he'd ever seen.

"You were saying, Miss...?" he asked as he watched the water lapping against her shoulders. When he heard his monotoned voice he knew he should be pulling himself out of the sensual haze he'd wandered into, but the struggle just didn't seem worth it. The movement of that bright blue water against her lightly tanned shoulders was drawing him back to the scene a few minutes ago when water was splashing against her bottom. That firm yet lush posterior that set off bells inside his head. And a need to pull at the knot in his tie as the scene settled into his consciousness. He dragged a finger across his mouth to hide his dry swallow, then shoved both hands in his pockets.

Resting against the pool wall, the woman positioned her chin on her stacked fists on the inside edge. "*Tsk, tsk.* I can't believe, after all we went through, that you would forget me so easily."

He narrowed his eyes as he fought back a wave of uneasiness. Although he'd never gone long without the touch of a woman, he wasn't one to indulge in lost weekends with them, either, so that possibility was out. But somewhere in time they'd shared an emotional moment or two. He rolled his eyes at her killer grin. When she turned it full force on him, suddenly it was the only thing he could think about. That and the relentless way she kept staring at him. She was a stubborn one all right. Flexing his knees, he frowned. Stubborn? Where had that stray thought come from? If he had to describe her he'd use words like charming. Delightful. Desirable. Mysterious. Definitely mysterious. No, he didn't remember her but he sure as hell would like to.

Shrugging, he gave her a help-me-out-here scowl. "I'm trying."

"Well, try harder...*Mr*. Hanlon," she said, raising her chin in a half-challenging, half-amused move.

He had to hand it to her. Most people would not have put up with his brusque manner, but she appeared to be feasting on it. Whoever she was, she had confidence to spare. And a directness that suggested the teasing light in her eyes wasn't simply a manifestation of her good humor.

"Let's see," he said, as the playful moment resonated with erotic overtones. "Would this memory I'm attempting to retrieve involve clothing?"

Her unrestrained laughter had him smiling.

"It's my hair."

He squinted. He was more confused than ever. He would have sworn "it" was her bottom. He had the distinct feeling he'd seen that flawless, neatly rounded, slim-hipped backside before. Or maybe he'd only imagined a tush as perfect as hers, but he wouldn't bet his tenure on it. "Your hair?" He shook his head. "I don't think it's your hair."

She reached to pull a few wet locks upward off her forehead. "I used to have it blond and spiked up on top."

Blond. Spiked on top. Raleigh looked at her hair and then her face. He drew in half a breath through his parted lips before the haze cleared and the earth shuddered to a stop. Cold prickles tumbled down his back. He slowly pulled his hands from his pockets. No. She couldn't be. He closed his eyes then dragged his hands over his face before he looked at her again. There it was, that wide-eyed, too-innocent smile. Air rushed from his lungs in a tortured groan.

The hair was different, the voice a little deeper, but her eyes hadn't changed. Big, blue and deceptively inno-cent…until it appeared she would never blink them. But back then he'd made it his business to make her blink. Those thickly fringed, brazen blue eyes that had chal-lenged his sanity more times than he could count, be-longed to the bane of his high school teaching career. So what if ten years had passed…he'd just been ogling one of his students. And not just any student! "Rebecca Barnett."

Her laughter shot through him like a well-aimed tickle, charging along nerve endings and into places it had no business going. It took effort not to smile at her genuine delight, but he was a master at disguising his emotions. Unfortunately he couldn't do anything about the unbidden and entirely unwelcomed thrill coursing through him.

Who knew where she could have taken this moment, if he hadn't figured out who she was? Lord help him. Who knew where he would have allowed, or worse, en-couraged her to take it? He swallowed hard as several interesting possibilities burgeoned into his conscious-ness. Heat continued building in his groin, testing the limits of his well-practiced composure. How long had it been since he'd indulged himself with ideas as wild as those?

Irritation suddenly got the better of him. Smoothing his palms along his thighs, he felt his nostrils flare.

"Still the same old games, Miss Barnett?" he asked, knowing full well that no matter what had just transpired, there had never been a hint of flirtation in their dealings as teacher and student.

Her laughter dissolved to a stunned look that grabbed at his gut. The playful light drained from her eyes and with it the easiness she'd brought to the encounter. He deserved a swift kick for that stupid remark.

"You know, you could have slipped on the diving board or hit your head on the bottom," he said, softening his tone as he lowered himself to his haunches. He laced his fingers together then let his hands dangle by the juncture of his thighs while he waited for her response.

Whether it was a wayward moment of guilt or the beginning step in a slow waltz of seduction, her gaze dropped to his wing tip shoes before traveling slowly to his mouth and then his eyes. She looked at him so long he began to think he was the one in danger of drowning.

"Christmas is coming. Where's your holiday spirit?" she asked, breaking the stare as she plowed more hair from her forehead.

The action caused a generous portion of her breasts to rise out of the water. He caught sight of the tight and tempting twin rosettes of flesh before she repositioned her body against the wall of the pool. Too late; he was already remembering the pale expanse of her belly, the dark thatch below and the sensations they'd caused in him.

He rubbed at his brow with his thumbnail as he tried to locate one cell in his body that wasn't being affected by her. Although Rebecca Barnett had never been easy to reason with in her high school days, at least she hadn't complicated their exchanges with enough sexual sparks to blow up the high school. Pursing his lips in a thoughtful manner, he drew on his dominant role as teacher.

"If I remember correctly, you usually pulled these stunts with a few friends in tow."

Twisting on the balls of his feet, he looked toward the gate, more to keep his gaze from tracing her delicate collarbone and the soft swells beneath it than to search for anyone else.

"So tell me, Miss Barnett, are we to expect another naked swimmer here anytime soon?"

From the corner of his eye he detected a slight change in her posture, a definite reangling of her chin and, finally, a lowering sweep of her lashes. His heart sank with the knowledge that he'd set something off inside her. A move he was sure he was going to regret.

In a voice thick with smoke and honey, she purred, "Not unless you're volunteering, Mr. Hanlon."

His gaze shot straight to hers. Everything he'd been trying not to think about poured into his mind and spilled over into his body. The moment hung hot and heavy between them until she had the grace to look away first. She scratched at the side of her nose.

"Oops. Am I getting detention for that one?"

Bracing his hands on his knees, he stood up. "Not this week," he said, going along with the joke because there was no way he couldn't.

The days were long gone when he could deal with her mischief by banishing her to detention. So were the days when he viewed her as a pretty, pain-in-the-butt teenager, a rebellious spirit who provoked him and the rest of the high school faculty as often as she could. Her self-confidence remained, though, tempered by ten years of experiences he couldn't begin to guess at. Except that those ten years had closed a gap between student and teacher. He went for her towel then took it to the side ladder.

"Am I getting evicted?" she asked, her body still hugging the wall as she pulled herself along the edge toward the ladder.

He draped the towel over the curved rail then turned to look at her.

"Not yet," he said in the threateningly quiet tone he used with his college students. Professorial intimidation usually put a stop to any of their shenanigans, but Rebecca Barnett's next teasing question told him, she wasn't buying it.

"Am I getting to you, Mr. Hanlon?"

He stepped closer to the edge. "Miss Barnett," he said, hoping to sound as dismissive as possible. "I assume by the looks of things that this mischief is a one-shot deal."

"Unless you've got a pool heater, I—"

"I don't," he said, leaning forward and planting his hands on his knees, this time to bring his face closer to hers. "The game's over. Let's call this a draw. Your lips are turning blue."

She pressed her collarbone closer to the wall and rolled her eyes. "That's not all that's turning blue," she said, before scrinching up her mouth in an exaggerated frown.

He looked away, not daring to allow his stare to stray to those buttocks he'd been admiring a few minutes ago.

"To answer your original question, I'm back in town early because I'm having a faculty get-together tonight. If you're planning to stay down here much longer I would appreciate it if you didn't walk by my windows naked on your way upstairs."

She batted her lashes at him. "Why is that?"

"Because ... Dean Callahan has a heart condition."
He turned to go, hoping to make a swift and decisive exit
before he made a complete fool of himself. Not too fast,
not too slow. A normal pace, as if he were leaving his
lecture hall. Then he heard the rush of disturbed water
and pictured her climbing out of the pool. The five remaining steps up to the gate turned into the longest walk
of his life.

"Mr. Hanlon. Wait up."

"We can finish this conversation later." As his hand
closed over the gate handle, he heard her bare feet slapping against cement. "Don't run!" Or I might have to
look at you completely naked. No pool wall, no distor-
tion from the water. Just perfectly and lusciously naked. Naked enough to blow my plan to treat you like the
rebellious seventeen-year-old student you insist on playing.

A sigh of relief rushed from him a split second after
she came into view. She'd managed to wrap the towel
around her and was tucking a corner between her
breasts.

"Yes, Miss Barnett?" he asked, watching her swipe
water from her chin with the backs of her fingers.

"How's *your* heart, Mr. Hanlon?"

Her clever response reminded him of the way she'd
always loved getting in the last word. *Brava.* Slipping his
hands in his trouser pockets, he nodded with a deceptively polite smile.

"Same condition it was in when we last spoke. Colder
than ever, Miss Barnett."

Now was the moment for making his getaway, but her
plucky attitude compelled him to wait for the inevitable
comeback.

"I've...ch-changed," she said as an impish grin teased at her lips.

Or was that a muscle twitch brought on by the cold?

He had all he could do not to reach out and give her arms a brisk rub. Knowing that wasn't the whole truth, he allowed his gaze to slide slowly down her body to the fine gold chain encircling her ankle. For some off-the-wall reason he couldn't fathom, the simple piece of jewelry inspired him to wonder how she would respond if he pulled her hard against him and kissed her until her lips were pink and swollen. If he gave himself half a chance he'd be putting the teacher/student taboo in the same place she obviously had. Ten years in the past. But he didn't believe in taking chances, even half of one.

"Here," he said, removing his jacket and wrapping it around her shoulders. "If you insist on prolonging this conversation," he said sternly, "I don't want you keeling over from hypothermia."

As he turned up the collar, she hunched her shoulders and pressed her cheek to it. His thumb brushed her mouth at the same time she exhaled a soft "ahh." The sound, coupled with the feel of her cool lips and puff of warm air, effectively bolted him to the flagstones beneath his feet.

Her eyelids drifted shut.

His lips parted.

"That feels so good," she said, luxuriating in the body heat clinging to the lining.

His body heat. His jacket. Her body. She was pushing buttons and jiggling toggle switches he didn't know he possessed until that second.

She flexed her knees and the subtle move made him think about her hips. He pictured the sleek curves, along with the rest of her body, brushing against the coat lining. The blatantly sensuous movement had him aching to pull her close and move with her. But he wasn't going to. No matter that he had his hands on a nearly naked woman with an arousingly sensual nature, he had distance to keep along with his sanity. He looked down at her rosy cheeks, her moist lips and the way her lashes clumped together to make little points. As the wind rustled the branches of a nearby holly tree, he reminded himself to breathe while he figured out what *not* to do next.

She wriggled closer. Or was he pulling her closer? Her eyes opened, locking with his gaze instantly. Unlike his heartbeat, her lashes had stopped fluttering.

"Mr. Hanlon," she whispered.

"Yes, Miss Barnett?"

"I—I'm not your student anymore and I—"

"I'm beginning to realize that," he said, taking in the treasures of her face.

She moistened her lips with a quick lick, leaving them wet, ready and quivering. He slid his thumbs down the lapels and took a step closer.

"Your point being . . . ?" he asked, his voice a husky drawl he hardly recognized as his own.

"I'll be right across the driveway from you. And you'll be . . . right across the driveway from me . . ."

He raised his eyebrows, urging her to continue with the simple but promising scenario.

"I'll be here through the holidays and the class reunion. And I was wondering if we—"

He let go of the lapels and stepped back. She was in town for her class reunion? What the hell was he doing! Counting and recounting the five freckles across her nose? Memorizing the little hum her body made when she sighed? Wondering who put that ankle bracelet above those pretty pink enameled toenails of hers? "The reunion. Of course. I see. And you'll be getting together with some of your old classmates. What is it that you want from me? Permission to throw a party? Maybe look the other way if you want another dip in the pool with your friends?"

She shook her head. "I want you to stop calling me Miss Barnett."

"You're married?" he asked, feeling strangely disappointed and relieved in the same moment.

"No," she said. "I just don't see the need, after all this time, for us to be so formal." She glanced down at her scanty attire. "Especially now."

He didn't even try to stop his smile. "You want me to call you Rebecca? Is that it?"

She thought for a moment. "No. Call me Reb."

"Reb? Why that old nickname? Why not Becky?"

Her gaze wandered over his face. "I just want to hear you call me Reb."

He nodded. "Short for rebel, wasn't it?"

Her shivers had stopped and her lips were curving into a quirky, lopsided smile that made his heart thump. "I think there'll always be a part of me that is," she said, hitching up her towel. "But just a little part...Raleigh."

"Raleigh?" He nodded as he spotted her gate key sitting on top of a security lamp. Handing it to her, he began working his own key out of the gate lock. "I'd prefer that over *my* old nickname."

"Old nickname?" she asked.

"You know, Reb, the one you stuck me with."

Her brows shot up in feigned innocence. "I have no idea what you're talking about."

"Sure you do. Show-No-Mercy Hanlon. You painted it on the wall in the teachers' lounge. In big green letters, as I recall."

"It wasn't in green, it was in red." A second later she was slapping a hand over her mouth and squeezing her eyes shut.

When more of his own memories about that incident began rushing in, he headed out of the gate and across the crushed stone drive.

"Mr. Han—I mean, Raleigh. Ouch! Wait!" she called as she hurried after him.

Turning to face her, he cleared his throat at the improbable sight before him. She was holding the jacket closed with one hand and gesturing with the other as she made her way across the stones. Her torturous progress resembled a sexy new dance step. The faster she moved the higher the hem of the jacket rose, exposing a widening line of terry cloth.

"I'm listening." *And looking. Lord, how I'm looking.*

Stopping abruptly, she attempted a wobbly balance as she jammed her free hand to her hip. Any hair that wasn't clinging to her head was framing her wincing expression in peaked, curvy locks.

"What made you think it was me who painted that—that name on the wall?" she asked, her tone both disbelieving and demanding. "We all wore ski masks that morning."

"You mean other than that you just confirmed it?" he asked, as he watched her towel begin sliding from beneath his jacket.

"Yes, of course, other than that," she said, gesturing emphatically, then frantically grabbing for the red terry cloth.

Too late, Raleigh thought, as the towel slid to her ankles over the most beautiful legs and backside he'd ever seen. "You mooned me then, too."

Two

Twenty minutes later Rebecca Barnett pushed open the door to the Chocolate Chip Café. Her gaze swept the interior of Follett River's favorite college coffee house, before zeroing in on the busy blonde behind the counter. Just the person she came to see, Reb thought as she made her way through the sea of tables to the counter. Moving one of the tall chairs aside, she pressed her hands on the faux marble surface and leaned toward her friend on the other side.

"Raleigh Hanlon's back in town."

Megan Sloan scooped a dollop of frosting from the bowl next to the three-layer cake on the counter. As the pretty young widow carefully spread the liqueur-scented mixture over the top, she raised her brows.

"Surprised you, did he?"

"You could say that," Rebecca said, sliding onto a cane-back chair as she shoved both sets of fingers through her damp hair.

"Reb, I tried calling you earlier to tell you, but I guess you haven't hooked up your answering machine yet. Aren't you concerned you'll miss your business calls?" Megan asked as she swirled the spatula through the frosting.

"New Horizon Tours' Miami office is more than capable of taking care of itself. That's why I'm thinking about opening a branch up here."

Megan Sloan checked the depth of frosting on the sides of the cake before finally looking up at her friend. Her green eyes widened. "Reb! Your hair!" she said, dropping the spatula into the bowl, then reaching for her friend's hands. "What have you been up to?"

"Do you want the whole story or just the good parts?"

"The whole story, of course," she said glancing at her watch. "And I bet it's a Barnett classic, but unfortunately I barely have time for the good parts. Piece Of Cake got a last-minute catering job that I couldn't pass up. So...?"

Nodding, Rebecca looked around to make certain no one was within earshot. No use blowing her new-and-improved image in front of a roomful of strangers, too. "I went skinny-dipping in Raleigh Hanlon's pool...and he caught me."

Megan choked back a scream. "Oh, Reb," she said, pulling napkins from a dispenser then shoving them against her mouth. When her fit of laughter slowed, she dabbed at her eyes and shook her head. "I'm so glad you came back to Follett River. Things have been darn dull since you left."

"Dull?" she asked, coming off the chair. "How could they possibly be dull with Raleigh Hanlon around?"

"Come on, it's been ten years since you two had those go-arounds. He's not so bad. Maybe a tad grumpy at times for someone in his thirties, but honestly—"

"I'm not talking about his grumpy side. I'm talking about his, well..." Her words trailed off as she pictured the way he looked at her as he wrapped her in his jacket. When he pulled the wool tweed collar against her cheek the sensation was surprisingly pleasant. A slow smile lifted one side of her mouth. And for a moment, there, so were you, Raleigh Hanlon.

"Yes? His...?" Megan urged as she began sprinkling chopped hazelnuts over the cake.

"Never mind," she said, easing her rear onto the seat again. The very rear she'd exposed to him on at least two different occasions. She took a deep breath then slowly exhaled at that last thought. "What's he been doing for the past ten years?"

Megan kinked a brow. "Why this interest in your least favorite teacher all of a sudden?"

Rebecca picked up a few pieces of chopped hazelnuts with the pads of her fingers. "No reason," she said before licking her fingertips and shrugging. "He's my landlord. That's all."

"You never could lie to me," her friend said in a singsong fashion.

"Meggie, give me a break here," she said, dropping her shoulders. "For old times' sake, just answer the question."

"I've already told you. He's a history professor at Follett College now. He's working on his second book about ancient civilizations. I think this one's about the Incas."

"Megan Sloan," Reb said in a tone reserved for mis-behaving pets, bad drivers and best friends who weren't getting the message. "I meant his private life."

Megan reached for a container of chocolate-dipped hazelnuts and began circling the top of the cake with them. "You know he's from over in Daleville. Well, about nineteen years ago his brother got a girl preg-nant, then died before he could marry her. Mr. Han-lon's been helping them out over the years. This niece, her name's Penny, is all he has left since both his par-ents are dead. Lately Penny has been giving her mother fits."

Rebecca tapped her nails on the faux marble as her friend went on about the girl's troublesome adoles-cence.

"Megan, I know all about how difficult teenagers can be. I believe I was the poster child for that particular condition five years in a row. What I want to know about is his *private* private life."

Setting aside the container, Megan rested her elbows on the counter and dropped her chin into the cups of her hands.

"Reb Barnett, what scandalous vengeance are you planning to wreak on poor old Professor Hanlon now?"

"Old? He's not old, he's—'' What was she defending him for? He'd left her standing in his driveway with her hard-won image of a mature woman, not to mention a bath towel, around her ankles. None of her reactions had made any sense then, and they weren't making any more sense now.

"Meggie," she said quietly, rubbing her temples, "I'm trying to sort out a few things."

"What things?"

"I don't know. He looked at me in an odd way."

"Gee, you don't think that had anything to do with him discovering you swimming naked in his pool, do you?"

Staring at the packages of gourmet coffees behind her friend, Rebecca absently ran her tongue over the edges of her teeth. "I think that was part of it."

Megan pushed up from the counter. "You're not joking, are you? Something's going on between you two, isn't it?"

Her friend's last question sounded like an indisputable fact and a disturbing one at that. The idea of being attracted to her former teacher was still an outrageous one to her, too. Opening her hands and raising them palms up, she gave an exaggerated shrug. "Nothing is going on. I just saw the man for the first time in ten years and ..."

"Sounds to me as if you just saw the *man* for the first time. What are you planning in that deliciously devious mind of yours?"

Rebecca gave a quick look around at the young college crowd hunched over their cappuccinos and caffé lattes before turning back to Megan. Scissoring her hands over the cake, she announced, "I have *never* thought of him in that way."

"Well, thank goodness for that," Megan said, in a deceptively demure voice. Lifting the cake, she placed the holiday dessert into a prefolded box then winked at her friend. "Because knowing you, you could have gotten him arrested."

"Very funny," she said, helping with the flapping box top. "I hope you don't think I'm thinking of him in that way today ..." The sound of her own nervous laughter made her wince. "I mean ... that's so ..."

"Ah, Reb, you used to be so articulate when it came to Mr. Hanlon. Now you can't seem to put together a complete sentence about the guy." She pressed her palm to her chest. "Did I mention he's divorced?"

"Divorced?" Reb repeated, unable to ignore how instantly hungry she was for more information. And how suddenly hesitant she was to ask for it.

"Four years ago, so I think we can safely say she's out of the picture. But imagine what his wife would have said if she'd found you naked in—"

"Dear Lord, I never considered the possibility that he could be married," she whispered.

"Really? Well, the important thing now is to think of him as available."

Available? The idea that she would be romantically interested in Show-No-Mercy Hanlon wasn't even funny. It was crazy.

"I swear, Meggie, that skinny-dip meant nothing more than a little secret revenge for all he put me through ten years ago. Now that I've seen him . . . now that he's seen me, all I want to do is prove to him that I've changed. That I can handle myself in a mature fashion," she said, her voice rising as she did from the stool. "That I'm not the self-indulgent, trouble-making heathen he once thought I was. That I'm dependable, presentable and charming as hell," she said, whacking her hand on the countertop. "What are you smiling about?"

"You're serious about that?"

"Damn straight," she said, flicking back an errant lock of hair that had tumbled over her forehead.

"Great. Then you can start demonstrating all those admirable qualities to him tonight."

"What do you mean?" she asked, kinking one brow.

"Raleigh Hanlon called me from Daleville this morning and asked if Piece Of Cake could cater desserts for a get-together at his place. I guess he's been so busy with his niece he'd forgotten he'd agreed to host the faculty's first holiday party. You'd be helping me out if you'd take this job. You see, I have umpteen calls to make for the reunion committee and I'd already promised Paige I'd teach her Chickadee group how to make pine cone Santas tonight."

"Wait, wait, wait. You want me to serve cake to a bunch of professors?" Rebecca asked, picturing her usually glib tongue tied in self-conscious knots. The thought of so many graduate degrees under one roof was beyond intimidating when she thought of the simple high school diploma she almost didn't receive.

"You'll have the undying gratitude of my five-year-old."

"Guilt can move mountains, Megan, but I don't know..."

"Reb, just think, you'll have the opportunity to impress Raleigh Hanlon...with all your clothes on this time."

An hour later Rebecca stood at Raleigh Hanlon's back door with his jacket around her shoulders. She was hugging a huge poinsettia plant to one hip and holding a shopping bag in her left hand. With her right she tinkered with the black bow tie her friend insisted had to be worn with the official Piece Of Cake caterer's uniform. The slender grosgrain ribbon wrapping primly around the starched stand-up collar of the pleated tuxedo shirt was the last thing Raleigh Hanlon would expect to see her wearing. She looked down at the rest of the uniform. The red plaid cummerbund and black, pleated trousers actually looked kind of cute. Cute? She winced. She was about to walk into Show-No-Mercy Hanlon's house looking cute. "Reb Barnett," she whispered, as she knocked on the door a second time, "if the old gang could see you now."

A second later the door opened and, without looking up, Raleigh was waving her in. He was speaking with considerable emotion into the telephone wedged between his shoulder and chin.

Rebecca remained on the doorstep taking in the details of the man who was totally absorbed in his conversation. His burgundy-and-blue tattersall shirt was rolled up at both wrists, exposing his Swiss Army watch and his handsomely muscled forearms. Unlike her miniature bow tie, his long navy blue one draped either side of his unbuttoned shirt framing a healthy amount of dark, crinkly chest hair. As if to counterpoint the vibrant signs of his masculinity, a pair of tortoiseshell reading glasses were perched near the end of his nose. Biting back a smile, she thought about what fun she could have had with those glasses ten years ago.

"I can't agree with you more, sweetheart," he said as he glanced at the paper in his hands. "But, Penny, I don't think your mother's being unfair about your curfew. I—don't hang up, young lady. Damn—!" He clicked off the phone and placed it firmly on the wall hook.

"Megan, I'm glad you're here—" His harried expression changed to a blank one the moment he saw who it was. Hesitating, he strained for a look over Rebecca's shoulder before refocusing on her uniform. "Is this one of your practical jokes?"

Jokes! Maybe this wasn't her leather miniskirt and combat boots from ten years ago, but she wasn't naked, either. Brushing back a lock of hair from her forehead, she swallowed hard and reminded herself that she was here to demonstrate the new and improved Rebecca Barnett. Nothing he could say would cause her to become unglued. Her gaze dropped to the opening of his shirt. As for that hairy chest of his . . . that might take considerably more restraint than she'd prepared for.

"I volunteered for this job when I found out Megan had made plans with her daughter," she said, aware that that wasn't exactly how she came to be standing on his doorstep. Lowering her gaze further down the front of him, she felt it melt into a genuine stare when she got to the dark whorl of hair above his navel. Blinking her way out of the hypnotizing sight, she made herself look at his face again. "I had to come back across town, anyway."

Resting a fist on his hip, he lowered his chin to deliver a challenging stare over his reading glasses. "Is that so?"

She tapped her nails against the red-foiled flowerpot and narrowed her eyes. Her voice was suddenly stronger. "I live here. Remember?"

"And you're working for Megan Sloan now?"

There it was again: that skeptical edge to his voice that said he wasn't sure about any of this. That maybe there was more she wasn't telling. And perhaps a trip to the principal's office might be in order.

With a long-suffering sigh, she answered him. "Just for tonight. And you can stop sounding so concerned. I haven't pebbled the cookies."

He waited five thoughtful seconds before he appeared to succumb to the inevitable. Folding the sheet of paper he'd been holding, Raleigh slid it in his shirt pocket. The action managed to tug his shirt sideways, exposing a flat, dark nipple surrounded by another whorl of dark hair.

"Of course you haven't pebbled the cookies, but Megan knows exactly how I like these things done. Not too formal—"

"She explained everything to me. So if you'll get those desserts and the containers from the van," she said, whipping his jacket from her shoulders and shoving it against his naked midsection, "I'll get started."

Closing a hand over the bunched tweed, he gave her a stiff nod. "Dining room's through that door over there."

Even though she'd managed to cover the tempting sight of his well-muscled, hair-roughened chest and abdomen, achy heat was already pooling between her thighs. Making an effort to appear unfazed, she breezed by him into the dining room.

"You are not going to get to me, Hanlon," she murmured to herself as she plunked the poinsettia on the credenza and pulled a tablecloth out of the shopping bag. Giving the rectangle of white damask a snapping shake, she spread it over the table, then began smoothing it into place. "So what if you happen to have mankind's most gorgeous chest and nipples that make my fingers itch? The idea of you and me ever . . . it's . . . just impossible," she said to herself in an angry whisper.

But as she kept picturing his exposed chest, her efficient moves to straighten the cloth slowed then stopped. Tilting her head, she stared at the white-on-white design in the tablecloth. The soft, lustrous swirls reminded her of the patterns in his chest hair. Tracing one swirl and then another with the pads of her thumbs, she began imagining the rougher texture of his hair, the heat of his skin below and the steady thumps of his heartbeat. When she realized she was holding her breath, she drummed both sets of fingers against the cloth **and** shook her head. She *really* had to start dating again now that her tour business was doing so well. Pushing up from the table, she reached for the potted red flowers and plunked them on the center.

With more determined effort, she went looking for dessert plates. While she was kneeling beside the opened credenza door, Raleigh came into the room.

"I put everything but this in the kitchen," he said over the cake box. "Finding everything you need in there?"

"I think so," she said, stopping to watch him settle a cake box on the table. In an unguarded moment he lifted the lid and leaned down for a quick sniff. Closing his eyes, he took a longer one. His obvious pleasure mesmerized her, then quickly made her blink. Of course, everyone had a sensual side, she'd just never thought about *him* having one.

Biting back a smile, she reached inside the credenza. "Megan said the dessert plates are supposed to be in here, but all I keep pulling out are these old photo albums."

Raleigh dropped the lid over the cake, then quickly kneeled beside her. "I'll take those," he said, removing them from her grasp and setting them out of her reach.

Before she had time to lower her hands, he was ducking his head near her lap to peer inside the credenza. Her heart skipped a beat and then another. Minutes ago she wasn't sure he was going to allow her into his house; now he'd positioned his face inches from the most intimate part of her anatomy. His clean male scent, mixed with his light, woodsy after-shave only added to the stunning immediacy of the moment. She held her breath as visions of them tangled together on the floor moved through her mind. In this position it would be so easy to sink her fingers into his hair and...

"Here we go." Pushing aside a soup tureen, he pulled out two stacks of gold-rimmed, red dishes. "Twenty ought to do it." Moving back on his heels, he set the dessert plates on top of the furniture then stood up.

"Well, thank you," she said, forcing herself to stare at the albums on the floor while she waited for her heart to reestablish a normal rhythm. Before that medical miracle had time to happen he took her hands, still raised in midair above her thighs, and pulled her to her feet.

When he held on a few seconds longer than necessary, the courteous act began snowballing into something altogether different. She tried telling herself it was the casual way his unknotted tie slid over her hands that gave the moment its intimate feel. The sensation of fine quality wool on her skin reminded her of a caress. Gentle. Masculine. And, because it had been ages since she'd had a lover, leaving her wanting more. She looked up as he looked away.

"My cleaning lady stored those albums in there by mistake," he said, still inexplicably holding on to her hands.

The oxygen in her body seemed to be disappearing— probably feeding those sparks zipping up her arms, through her heart, into her stomach and then, heaven help her, even lower. He looked back at her as she parted her lips to draw in an extra breath.

"Are you all right?" he asked, letting go of her hands to place his around her elbows.

"I'm fine . . . just stood up too fast," she said, fighting the compelling desire to lean her cheek against his chest and her forehead against that tuft of hair *where he still hadn't finished buttoning his shirt!*

"Back to work," she announced, reaching for the first stack of plates with shaky hands. Why wasn't he saying something? Or moving away? Or taking her in his arms and kissing her silly? She squeezed her eyes shut. Was she losing her mind? What had gotten into her? Tonight was her opportunity to show him she'd changed.

"Yes, back to work," he finally said, as he leaned down to pick up the photo albums from the floor. "I have more notes to go over before people start arriving."

"Don't let me bother you." She kept her eyes on the gold circle rimming the red plate in her hand as he walked into his library.

For the next twenty minutes she kept herself busy by folding napkins, preparing coffee, mixing the cranberry punch, setting out the dessert buffet and pretending that what she'd felt when he'd been so close was nothing more than a fluky moment of hormonal insanity.

After setting a pitcher of milk on the table next to a matching sugar bowl, she glanced across the hall into the library where Raleigh paced before the fire. He'd put on music, a Bach concerto, if she wasn't mistaken. As he read through his paper, she found herself pressing her hand to her midsection. If what she'd felt was nothing more than one fluky moment of hormonal insanity, why were her hands still tingling? Her throat still dry? And that disturbing heat still pooling where it shouldn't be? After all these years what was it about him that she suddenly found so compelling?

She walked across the carpeted hall to the open pocket doors of the library. Without a doubt he was an attractive man. Standing well over six feet, he was broad shouldered, classically handsome and, unlike most indoor career types, sporting a healthy tan. His thick, dark hair threatened to spill over his forehead in a little-boy tousle of loose curls.

As he braced a hand on the mantel and worried over his paper, she folded her arms, leaned her shoulder against the doorjamb and quietly sighed. Who the heck was she kidding? Raleigh Hanlon was the best-looking man she'd ever laid eyes on. And there he was, in his leather-bound, gold-stamped library, so absorbed in his professorial studies that he didn't even sense her presence.

Angling her head into the room, she strained to take in his floor-to-ceiling, book-lined shelves, his leather wing chair with the worn spot where he rested his head, and his framed degrees and certificates filling half a wall. Masculinely appointed, impressively erudite and with a tried-and-true sense of permanency, the room appeared to be a perfect representation of the man standing in it. And just as awesome to her.

She nibbled on her lip as that unwelcome sense of inadequacy sent a cold tentacle to her stomach. Before the feeling took a stronger hold, she stood up and lifted her chin. Even if her poor high school performance had kept her out of college, over the last ten years, through hard work and pure determination, she had managed to achieve just about everything else she'd wanted in her life. She had nothing to be ashamed of.

"I set aside a piece of cake for you," she impulsively announced.

Against the Bach playing in the background, her voice sounded like a carnival barker's. She was certain Raleigh thought the same when he removed his glasses and looked up at her for a long, uncomfortable moment. Or maybe that look was meant for something else? Had she splashed the cranberry punch on her clothes? Had they fallen off? What was wrong?

The crackling flames in the fireplace were the only sounds she heard above her pounding heartbeat. And then he smiled. That funny, forgiving kind of smile that said everything was all right. The kind of smile she'd never seen on Show-No-Mercy Hanlon.

"Which cake?" he asked.

"The one you were sniffing," she said, relaxing enough to notice his shirt was finally buttoned and his tie knotted. "The hazelnut with the Frangelico frosting."

"Ah," he said, nodding slowly. "You don't miss much."

She smiled back as she let her gaze wander the room again. This time the place didn't feel as threatening. "Where's your Christmas tree?"

"Excuse me?"

"Your Christmas tree? The ceramic angels on the mantel? The candles in the windows?" Pointing upward she added, "The mistletoe? Megan said this was the first holiday party of the season, but it's hard to tell you've looked at the calendar."

He looked around before giving her a halfhearted scowl. "Isn't that poinsettia enough?"

She scowled back. "No," she said and they both laughed. As the sound died he kept on looking at her. When she didn't say anything, he slid on his reading glasses and lifted up his paper.

"That must be some interesting paper," she said, grasping at the mundane comment because she was already missing the moment they'd shared.

He brushed a piece of lint from the top of his pant leg then looked at her again. "I'm sure you wouldn't find it very interesting."

She forced a smile to cover the raw sting of his words. Was it so obvious to him that she hadn't furthered her formal education? "Maybe I would. Try me."

"Have you studied the history of the Incas?"

"Well, not formally," she said, raking her fingers through her hair. Why were her palms sweating? He wasn't giving her a test on the subject, but if he were, she would probably pass the darn thing with flying colors.

"Not formally?" he repeated, motioning for her to come in and take the chair by the fire. "What do you mean?"

"I've read a bit on my own," she said, wondering if she should tell him how many hours she'd studied pre-Columbian history before leading a tour group through the ruins at Machu Picchu and the archaeological dig site on the northwest coast of Peru. The last thing she wanted to do was sound as if she were bragging, or worse, defending herself.

Raleigh raised a brow as he watched her enter the room. "Amazing. When you were my student I practically had to glue a history book in your hands in order to get you to read it."

"That's a good ten years in the past."

Slowing her steps and her words, she stopped at the sofa table. As she reached down to it, Raleigh remembered what he'd left there. The yearbook of her graduating class was lying wide open to the page with her photo.

Her gaze, accompanied by a slow grin, darted up to him then back down again. "But I guess history professors have been known to spend a little time poking around in the past."

As she picked up the book, he turned away to check his watch. Fifteen minutes to eight. If he hadn't spent time poring over Rebecca's yearbook this afternoon he would have finished his work, he thought, going to his desk and dropping the paper into a drawer. But he *had* looked at the yearbook, and the rest of his day had been filled with thoughts about her. Thoughts leading to questions. Crazy questions that kept on coming when he pictured her naked in the pool, then standing beside him in that towel.

He looked over at her now, quietly smiling as she thumbed through the pages. She looked so…grown-up. He snorted softly. Maybe she was, but that didn't stop the questions he'd been thinking about all afternoon.

What in hell made you pull those crazy stunts in high school? Was I too hard on you? Wasn't I hard enough? How many hearts have you broken? What's happened to you since then? What's happened to me? And when did you turn into such a beautiful woman?

"Raleigh, why did you have this opened to my—?" she began at the same moment the doorbell rang.

He looked at her expectant expression as the doorbell sounded again, along with the telephone. The outward composure he'd been perfecting for the past eighteen years clicked into place.

"Would you mind getting the door and showing whoever it is into the library?" he asked, as he walked past her into the dining room. Picking up the plate of sliced cake she'd left for him, he added, "I'll take the phone in the kitchen."

Five minutes later Raleigh hung up. As Penny had railed on with her latest litany of teenage complaints, he'd found that his thoughts had kept wandering back to Rebecca. She'd been Penny's age when she was his student. He shook his head. Penny's age, for godsake.

Taking his jacket from where he'd tossed it, he remembered the way Rebecca had looked in it. Even though the salt-and-pepper tweed was sizes too big for her, he couldn't say she looked exactly childlike wearing it that afternoon. And when she'd bent down to catch her towel ... The distinct tugging sensation in his manhood had him swallowing dry. He quickly shrugged on the jacket then straightened his tie. He had guests waiting.

Picking up the cake she'd sliced for him, he dragged two fingers through the frosting, then plunged them into his mouth to lick them clean. Laughing at himself for the outlandish thoughts he'd been having about Rebecca, he lifted the whole slice from the plate and took a bite.

She'd once been capable of getting under his skin, but that was strictly sophomoric and a long time ago. She wouldn't be doing that again; he wouldn't let her. Shoving another bite into his mouth, he closed his eyes and savored the delicate flavor. Hell, he must have been crazy there for a few hours. He was years older than Rebecca, and, just as important, she was years younger than him. Coupled with their history, anything remotely ... adult was laughable.

As he reached to open the dining room door, Rebecca opened it from the other side. Her cheeks were flushed, her hair was slightly mussed and her high spirits a nearly tangible force. The beguiling sight almost made him forget his reassessment.

"Who rang the bell?" he asked, as she quickly closed the door behind her then leaned against it.

"Dean Callahan," she said, before covering her mouth to stop a burst of laughter.

"What's so funny?"

She pressed her hands against her bright plaid cummerbund and leaned forward to catch her breath. "Oh, Raleigh, I always thought professors were so stuffy, but that one's not. He wouldn't stop asking me questions about myself. I tried to explain that I was only here catering your desserts and he said, 'Well, I never heard it referred to as that before.'" Shaking her finger at him, she widened her eyes. "Your Dean Callahan is a very naughty man."

"Naughty?" He smiled at the thought that the white-haired gentleman could ever be considered naughty.

"Yes. Don't you get it?" she asked with an exaggerated wink.

"Don't I get what?" He felt his smile weakening while he silently prayed that the gods were with him tonight and what he was beginning to suspect was way off the mark.

She took a step toward him. "Oh, Raleigh, look at you," she said, changing subject and tone as she reached up to cup his jawline in her hands. "You have frosting smeared here...and here." Dabbing at the sides of his mouth with her thumbs, she squinted at him. "Look. Go like this."

Her helpful gesture almost made it into the casual category until she puckered her lips. His breath caught somewhere north of his chest. Hadn't he just convinced himself how ridiculous this illogical attraction he had for her was? Hadn't he told himself to get a grip? And didn't she have the softest hands and most engaging expressions?

He closed his hand around one of hers causing her fingertips to stray past his lips. Once. Twice. With her breasts brushing his chest, her gentle yet relentless thumb strokes and the liqueur-laced frosting teasing his tongue, he had all he could do not to lick her. Then her thumbnail grazed the underside of his lip, and her kind act began bordering on a kinky one. Taking a step over the line of common sense, he bypassed warm, fuzzy confusion and headed straight for the Pandora's box of heat and lust. Curving a hand around her waist, he tugged her against his hips. "Rebecca," he whispered. Then the doorbell rang again and both of them froze.

Crashing back to reality, Raleigh found himself staring into her eyes. He knew his boundaries; he'd set them up a long time ago. "You were saying something about Dean Callahan?" he asked, as he let go and took a step backward.

She gave him a puzzled look that, after a few nerve-jangling seconds, transformed itself into a focused, knowing smile. "He thinks I'm your latest."

"Latest what?" he asked as the doorbell rang again. He laughed out loud; this couldn't be happening. Where was a lesser god when you needed one?

"Lover." She cocked her head when he didn't respond. "Did you hear me? I said he thinks we're lovers."

"I heard you."

"Then why aren't you laughing anymore?"

He started around her. "Miss Barnett, I have to get the door—"

Her arm shot out, effectively blocking his way as she slapped her hand against the door frame. "And whatever happened to you calling me Reb? I thought we'd come so far, but—"

"Obviously, *we* haven't," he said, wondering why the hell he'd allowed her to put her hands on him in the first place.

"We haven't?" she asked, her head turning and her eyes twinkling with womanly mischief.

From the other side of the door, Dean Callahan called out cheerfully, "I'll get that."

"Miss Barnett, that will be all for tonight."

She opened her mouth to speak.

"Go," he said, then cocked his chin when she hesitated. As she walked around him and headed for the back door, his gaze tracked her like radar on enemy aircraft. He felt his body quickening to alert status when she paused with her hand on the knob. Looking over her shoulder at him, she made a new and old and needy ache start up in his heart.

"Raleigh?"

"Yes?"

She touched a fingertip to her lips. "You still have some..."

His hand began drifting up toward his mouth before he came to his senses and, instead, pointed at her. "Out! Now!" he said, managing to hold his ground even though the floor beneath him felt like quicksand when she grinned.

"Just like old times... *Mr.* Hanlon."

Her voice echoed through him, soft and sexy, sure and seductive. As she closed the door behind her, he slowly pressed his fingers to where hers had been. After a moment he shook his head and headed for the dining room. "Old times were never like this, Rebecca."

Three

As Raleigh fastened the last spring lock on the pool cover, he took another look toward the garage apartment. Two days had passed since that rub-and-tickle moment with Rebecca, and he was still battling over what to do about her. Ignoring her presence seemed like the most sensible and least bothersome solution, he decided, as he stored the pool equipment in the cabana. After all, how much trouble could one woman cause in a month? He seriously considered giving Rebecca the benefit of the doubt.

And then he came to his senses. She wasn't just any woman. She was Rebecca Barnett, complete with a shared history and enough sex appeal to melt the leather elbow patches off his tweed jackets. And she was living a few feet across the driveway from him.

Staring up at the apartment again, he came to the conclusion that while she might be able to stay out of trouble, *he* was the one with the problem. He couldn't ignore her presence because he couldn't put those moments with her in his kitchen out of his head.

Wiping his hands on his well-worn jeans, he headed for the gate. There was only one course of action he could take, he decided, as he closed it behind him. Rebecca Barnett would have to find alternative lodging. And as soon as he saw her—

"Finally got that pool closed, did you?"

She was sitting on the second-floor landing of the garage steps, a pair of mud-coated sneakers next to her feet. Her rosy cheeks made him think she'd been outside as long as he had, and her smile made him certain she'd been having more fun.

When he didn't answer her quickly enough, she thumbed up the suede brim of her baseball cap then leaned her elbows on the step behind her. Propping a sock-clad foot over one knee, she stared down at him. The jocklike posturing accentuated the length of her legs, the womanly curves of her hips and, where her athletic jacket fell open, the distinct pearling of her sweater-covered nipples in the cold afternoon breeze.

"Well, closing it's for the best, I guess." She shrugged. "Or who knows what I might have been tempted to do next down there."

Her smile said she was teasing but that didn't stop the images from coming into his head. Was there such a thing as nude ice-skating? He rubbed at his brow. This had to stop.

"It's best not to speculate," he said, walking over to the staircase. Resting a foot on the bottom step, he crossed his arms high on his chest.

"Look, about the other night. I apologize for being abrupt with you. There was no excuse for my behavior."

She leaned forward to rest her forearms on her knees. "Right, there was no excuse, but there must have been a reason."

One thing he could invariably count on, Rebecca Barnett always cut through the bull. Today her even stare and frank suggestion said she wouldn't settle for a polite lie or even the watered-down truth about his recalcitrant niece and his backed-up work on his manuscript. "I was still reacting to finding you like . . . I found you in the pool. Rebecca, maybe your staying here isn't such a great—"

"Hold on there," she said, raising a palm in his direction as she stood. Readjusting the fit of her jeans around her thighs, she dropped her chin to look at him. He'd lifted his gaze just in time to meet hers. "Have you got any of that cranberry punch left?"

"Cranberry punch? Yes," he said, wondering where she was taking this conversation.

"That will work."

"It will?"

"Sure. While you're thinking up a polite way to evict me, you can bring some up and I'll heat it in the microwave for us. I'm about to freeze out here."

Reaching behind her for the door, she lifted her face, closed her eyes and took a deep breath. "I swear, Raleigh, I can smell snow in the air."

Smell snow? He was having a hard time just breathing at the moment. Her short-cropped sweater had ridden up near her rib cage revealing her slim waist, and a firm and flawless midriff neatly punctuated with an outie.

"Can't you smell the snow?" she asked as if she didn't have cause to worry that he was about to kick her out in it.

He gave her a weak smile and a nod.

"I think if it snows this early we're more likely to have a white Christmas. Don't you agree? Raleigh?"

"White Christmas. Sure," he said, blinking as he looked away. He tended to ignore holidays. That was another reason for him to ask her to leave. If it didn't snow she'd probably cover the house with the artificial variety, play a tape of "Joy to the World" and dance naked around the holly bush in the front yard. Naked. Did he have to picture her naked again? He felt his shoulders droop. This time his scowl came with a determined shake of his head. "I'll be up with that punch in just a minute."

"Great," she said, stepping up as she pushed open her door. "I'll put the popcorn in the microwave."

"This is not a party," he said, raising his voice, but she'd already gone in and closed the door.

Less than five minutes later he was knocking on it, as he glanced at the plastic container of punch in his other hand. This *wasn't* going to be a party, just an opportunity to end her subletting on a cordial note.

His gaze shifted to her sneakers sitting on the edge of the step. How had she got them that muddy? he wondered. There hadn't been a rain storm or mud puddle in Follett River for weeks. Looking away, he knocked again, then rubbed his Saturday stubble as his gaze slid back to the shoes on the step. He snorted and shook his head. The last thing he needed to concern himself with was a pair of muddy sneakers. And how she'd got them that way.

The door came open and there she was, all welcoming smile and resonating energy. The first thing he could think to say was, "This is not a party."

With one hip pressed against the edge of the door and her hand braced against the frame, she began eyeing him. "Hmm. Let's see. You combed your hair. But you didn't shave. You're probably right. This isn't a party," she said, stepping back and waving him in. As he passed by her she leaned in close to his ear. "Just your average landlord-tenant eviction."

Her warm, cinnamon-scented breath and good humor made him smile in spite of his plan. Once inside the tiny kitchen he turned around to look at her. Her hands were behind her back holding on to the doorknob while she boldly continued to study him.

"All right, you're biting at the bit to say something. What is it?"

"You know, the last time I saw you in jeans and a sweatshirt you were standing next to the flag pole over at the high school lecturing me. Remember?"

A safe subject, thank the Lord, he thought, as he placed the punch on the kitchen table. "I do remember. It was snowing and you were upset about missing your class ski trip because I'd given you Saturday detention. You'd dragged your chair outside in protest, and no one could make you come back in. So they called me at home to see if I could persuade you."

"That's right," she said, bumping his hip as she brushed past him in the small confines of the kitchen. "Sorry." She reached into a cupboard for two mugs. When she set them on the table, he unscrewed the container and began filling them as she watched. "I can see you now, walking across that unbroken field of snow. You must have stayed there shivering for twenty minutes while you lectured me on what my futile protest was doing to my health.''

Raleigh glanced at her as he recapped the container. He was close enough to count her eyelashes, close enough to move a lock of hair off her forehead with one puff of air, close enough to detect her faint, womanly scent mixing with the tart, sweet cranberry smell. He took a calming breath. ''And do you remember what you told me?''

She bit down on her lip, trying hard not to laugh when the microwave dinged. ''Why don't you refresh my memory?'' she asked, as she took the popcorn out of the oven. Pinching open the bag, she emptied it into a bowl.

He moved around her and placed the filled mugs in the microwave. Shutting the door, he pushed a few buttons and when the machine began to hum, he turned to look at her. ''As I recall, you told me to blow it out my nose.''

Her laughter was deep and merry and so enchanting he raced to that far, safe place in his brain and fought off the urge to join her. The last thing he wanted was to encourage her. ''Were you always that . . . rebellious?''

She reached across the small space separating them and gave his forearm a playful squeeze. No one had touched him like that in a long time. He swallowed. She'd simply caught him off guard, and the effect was like an out-of-control pinball bouncing off his nerve endings.

''Raleigh!'' she said in a teasing scold. ''My teddy bear did not have a nose ring, if that's what you're thinking.'' Reaching into the bowl, she lifted out a handful of popcorn. ''And what about you?''

''Me?''

''Yes, were you always so suffocatingly cautious?''

"Don't you mean responsible?" he asked, as the face of his brother, Buddy, flashed through his consciousness.

"No," she said, throwing a piece of popcorn at him. "I meant cautious."

He cleared his throat and looked away from her when more thoughts of Buddy came into his mind. "I was known to raise a little hell. So did a lot of kids," he said as he finally looked back at her. "But I grew up."

The hum of the microwave seemed to get louder until she spoke. "So did I," she said, challenging him with a sure and steady stare.

"I noticed that about you out by the pool the other day," he said, hoping his brash reference to her nude swim would stop any questions she was about to ask.

"I thought you might have," she said, bumping her elbow against the door latch after the microwave dinged. Stepping away from the opening door, she picked up the popcorn and headed for the sun porch off the kitchen. "Why don't you bring those drinks out here?"

His reference to her skinny-dip had unnerved him more than it had her. Carefully carrying the mugs behind her, he said, "Dean Callahan mentioned that you're working at a tour agency in Miami. How long have you had that job?"

"I've been there almost seven years," she said, moving several rolls of Christmas wrapping paper off the rattan love seat and onto an end table. Tucking a leg beneath her, Rebecca settled into the far corner, placed the bowl of popcorn on her lap and reached for the mug he offered. "And I've owned it for the last four."

"You *own* it?" he said, hesitating before settling into his corner.

"You sound surprised," she said, feeling happier than she had any sane reason to.

"It's just...I had no idea you'd done so well for yourself." Turning to her, he scratched his chin. The masculine sound of his blunt nails scraping against his hair-roughened face brought a distinctly intimate feel to the moment.

"With my lousy grades and bad attitude when it came to my studies, I shouldn't be surprised you'd think that way about me. But I found something that I love doing. Something that suits parts of my personality." She offered him the popcorn, and when he waved it away, she cradled the bowl in her lap.

"What parts?" he asked turning himself to face her.

"The leader, organizer parts. The adventurous part. Whenever I speak to groups I make it clear that New Horizon's tours are not for the faint of heart. I always make sure there's a certain amount of adventure involved. I just got back from a month-long tour of South America," she said, before inhaling the cranberry-scented steam rising from her mug.

"That's pretty dangerous isn't it?"

"I wouldn't put anyone in danger. As a matter of fact, I waited until I was satisfied that the political situation was stable before offering that trip. That's why I was excited when Megan called about the class reunion she's been organizing. This trip back to Follett River was meant to be."

"Why do you say that?"

"My father died a year ago, and I try to get up here to see my mother as often as I can, but those quick, weekend trips aren't enough. I needed to do some business up this way, so I planned this trip over Christmas. The reunion was a bonus event, the cherry on top."

"So why aren't you staying with your family?" he asked, his tone more curious than judgmental.

"Well, I tried it for a couple of days," she said, placing the popcorn between them on the cushion. "But my sister and her three little ones moved in a few weeks ago. They're great kids. I just couldn't get any work done. I thought I might have to take a room at the Maxwell, but I spend so much time in hotels I wanted that to be a last resort. When Megan told me about this apartment being available through New Year's, it sounded like just what I need," she said, trying not to stare at the comfortable sprawl of his legs. Or the way his baby blue jeans softened yet defined the muscles in his thighs and the masculine ridge above them.

"What do you need?"

She looked toward the wall of windows as she tapped her finger against the mug in time with her heartbeat. "Living space for about a month. And a temporary office with an extra phone line for my fax machine. Megan's brother even has a separate line here that he was using for his modem," she said, standing up and moving toward the row of windows. "And I love that this is a quiet street yet so convenient to the downtown. From here you can see them decorating the center spruce for the tree lighting next week, and if you press your cheek against the window, you can get a glimpse of the river through those empty oak branches next to the campus." When she looked back at him she had the distinct impression that he'd never taken his eyes off her.

"So this visit is a working vacation for you," he said, lifting his mug to his lips.

She nodded. "I've been thinking about opening a branch office."

"Here in Follett River?" he asked, propping his elbow on the back of the love seat then resting his face against his hand.

His casual posture, mellow expression and friendly grin warmed her to the bone. He actually sounded interested, as one professional to another, about what she was doing.

"Yes. Isn't it amazing? I used to think Follett River was in the smack dab middle of nowhere," she said, sitting down beside him again. "Did you know that my most memorable quote for the yearbook was, 'Can't wait to blow this 'burb'?"

He nodded, confirming what she'd suspected when she'd discovered her yearbook in his library yesterday. He'd been curious enough about her to read the blurb beneath her photo and remember it. This was getting more interesting by the moment. "Anyway, there's not another travel agency in a fifteen-mile radius," she said, touching off her points with a thumb to her fingertips. "The college has grown over the last decade. The train stops here six times a day now. Demographically it looks like a smart move for my company."

"I see you've been thinking this through carefully. Do you have a specific place in mind?" he asked, stretching his arm along the rolled rattan until his hand was inches from her shoulder.

"I was looking at a possible site this afternoon. It's the old warehouse across the river."

His fingers curled around the blond rattan as his unguarded expression suddenly hardened. "You did what?" he asked, sitting up so quickly that the cranberry punch threatened to slosh over the top of his mug. He set the mug on the side table.

"I rode over to the old warehouse."

"The warehouse at the end of Rieger Street?"

"Yes. I heard a developer's negotiating to buy it and turn it into an office building. They're saying there's going to be room for a restaurant, and later they might rebuild the pier to dock a riverboat for sight-seeing."

"Rebecca Barnett, that might well be in the future, but right now the riverfront's a damned dangerous place. Anything could have happened to you. Are you aware there was a drug incident there this summer?"

She shook her head and sighed; she recognized that tone, that posture, that knitted brow, so well. Raleigh Hanlon was revving up for a vintage safety lecture, and until he finished she could do nothing but eat her popcorn and enjoy the show.

"There was, and someone was shot. And the dock's rotted through and . . ." Taking hold of one of her sock-clad feet where river mud had smeared, he lifted his other hand then dropped it to his knee. "Tell me you didn't walk out on it."

"A little way," she said, setting her mug on the floor.

"Half the boards are missing, and the pilings are loose. You could have fallen through. You could have broken a bone or worse."

"I'm fine. You see," she said, tapping her shoulder, "I've always had a guardian angel."

Pointedly ignoring her attempt to lighten the mood he was in, he continued. "Kids go down there with BB guns and shoot out the streetlights. You could have—"

"Is that so?" she asked, exaggerating her wide-eyed look as she moved closer.

"Yes, that's so," he replied adamantly.

"Why, Raleigh Hanlon, for someone who wants to evict my butt, you sound awfully concerned about saving it all of a sudden." Before he could respond, she went on. "And I didn't even tell you about the scary part."

He stared at her for a long, disbelieving moment. "Okay, what else were you up to?" he asked, arching a brow to the inevitable.

"You know that rope hanging from the steel girder by the loading dock? Back in high school there was one there, too, and Rory Buchanan and I used it to swing out over the river."

"Oh God, Rebecca," he said, rubbing his furrowed forehead. "Tell me you didn't do that today."

"I did, but when it came to jumping clear, I misjudged the height of the bank and ruined my sneakers. Would you like to see the rest of the damage?" she asked, setting the bowl of popcorn behind her and peeling off one sock. Stretching her leg over his thighs, she braced her foot on his armrest. As her calf rested on his thighs she could feel his hard muscles tense. Leaning forward, she was nose to nose with him as she rolled back the navy denim cuff. "If you look really hard you can see one itty-bitty bump right there on my ankle," she said, sliding her ankle bracelet half an inch up her shin. "Can you see it?"

"No," he said, gently rubbing his fingertips along her ankle bone. "But I didn't bring my glasses."

"Trust me. It's not worth wasting a bandage on," she said, as the pleasure from his touch streamed up her leg like bubbles in fine champagne. "It's barely a kiss-my-boo-boo bump," she added, wishing he would raise her leg a little higher and press his lips to her ankle, anyway. "I was fine."

"Fine," he repeated softly, before a frown of realization descended over his handsome face. Setting her leg away from him, he said, "You were not fine. You were lucky."

"Oh, Raleigh, if it were up to you, no one would ever have any fun," she said, maneuvering herself around until she was resting her derriere on her ankles. "What did you expect me to do when I came back to my old stomping ground? Stay tucked up in that curlicued brass bed in there and worry about meteors streaking out of the sky to bonk me," she said, softly rapping his head with her knuckles, "right there. Or there and there," she said, thumping his shoulders, one after another. When his only response was to fold his arms across his chest and stare across the room, she lowered her hands to her thighs.

At any time he could have easily moved out of her reach and back to the corner of the sofa. But he didn't. Spurred on by that, she inched forward until her knees were touching his thigh. The contact caused him to turn his face to her, and she could tell by his hooded eyes that he was waiting to see how far she would dare take things.

Shimmying her shoulders like an exotic dancer, she moved her face closer to his. "You've got to learn to loosen up."

"Rebecca..." His halfhearted warning sounded more desperate than edgy.

Shimmying her shoulders again, she laughed softly then touched her fingertips to the sides of his mouth. The abrasive feel of his stubble and the welcoming warmth of his skin were a double-strength magnet urging her closer. "Come on. I almost saw it. Raleigh, was that a smile?"

"You're playing a dangerous game here, young lady."

The message in his eyes was easy to read. She could move away now and all would be forgiven. Maybe even forgotten. But she wasn't looking for forgiveness, and she had no intention of forgetting this moment. Or of letting him forget it. Sliding her fingers up the sides of his face she leaned close.

"I know I am," she said, tilting her head to brush her lips against his. When he didn't respond, she brushed them again until his parted. When she broke contact, he took a long, determined breath and said her name again. Undaunted, she dipped her head for the third time, but stopped short of a kiss when she sensed a change in him. She started to take her hands away. "At least, I *thought* it was dangerous."

"You have no idea," he said, pulling her into his lap and taking her lips with a soft and sumptuous crush from his own.

The moment his arms touched her back and his fingers gently wound into her hair she knew this was not going to be a vengeful kiss. This was a rich, intoxicating and thorough kiss that was soon involving nibbles and licks and sexy promises she had every intention of holding him to.

Four

Raleigh was going to hate himself in the morning, but the feel of her in his arms, the taste of her on his lips and the welcoming way she was saying his name made an already tempting package impossible to resist. If only for the inconvenient pleasure of her impudent kisses. Long, deep, lush kisses tasting of cranberries and popcorn and the essence of Rebecca.

He'd meant to hold her steady until they satisfied her curiosity. And maybe a bit of his, too, he conceded, as his fingertips began straying past the bottom edge of her sweater. Then she twisted in his embrace, and the satiny texture of her skin began drawing him like a thirsty man to water. Her body was a brimming life force that couldn't be denied. Urging her closer became his only goal.

He whispered her name. She responded with a painfully sweet sound in the back of her throat. He whispered it again, and this time she held her breath as she bunched his sleeves in her fists. One tug and the kiss became the be-all and end-all of his existence. In the next second popcorn was spilling across the sofa and onto the floor as she began backing away.

"Don't go," he said, curving his hands around her bottom.

Hesitating for a second, she allowed him to guide her back to straddle his thighs. She moved over him, kissing him softly as she hovered above his lap like hot sunshine on a winter day. After a few heavenly seconds he realized the slow burn she was bringing to his groin wasn't hot enough. Grasping her hips, he brought her firmly down on the ridge of his straining fly.

Her sparkling eyes and dazzling smile told him she was as surprised as he was by the quickness and intensity of their response to each other. She laughed a soft, vital laugh as she slipped her fingers through his hair to cradle the back of his head.

"How dangerous did you want to make this?" she asked breathlessly.

A low warning signal sounded in the back of his mind, but he ignored it and instead lifted up with his hips. Her light laughter thickened to a gasp as he felt her thighs tightening around his. Reveling in her response, he repeated the provocative move. This time she closed her eyes in such an honest display of earthy sensuality it made him ache. Nothing this wrong had ever felt so right.

"Oh-h-h, Raleigh," she whispered, reaching beneath his sweatshirt. As she covered his mouth with a kiss wet and hungry enough to rival his own, her cool fingers were working magic on his heated flesh.

He'd never experienced any woman like her. Somewhere in this reckless game of dare and desire, she had chosen desire. Rich, wild desire that, whether she knew it or not, was reaching deep inside him and demanding more than a physical act. Demanding the one thing he couldn't deal with. That unmistakable feeling of vulnerability.

"Rebecca," he whispered against her lips.

"Yes," she managed between a lick and a nibble.

He resisted the urge to kiss her back. If he didn't stop now, he never would. "Look at me."

She pulled away just enough to focus her drowsy eyes on him.

"Rebecca, we can't do this," he said, fighting the longing to tumble her to the floor and taste every womanly inch of her.

"Why not?" she asked, her slightly upturned lips wet with his moisture.

No sense of disbelief. No timidity. Simply a straight-from-the-heart "Why not?" Her openness had him wishing for an instant he could take back what he'd just said. But only an instant, because that feeling of vulnerability was slipping in again.

Guiding her off his thighs, he settled her on the cushion next to them. He counted to ten before he pushed up from the love seat and walked over to the windows.

"I'm not going to stand here and insist there isn't a certain amount of attraction between us, but that's as far as this is going. You were my student, Rebecca. There's just no way," he said, slicing his hand through the air, "that I can forget that."

"I'd worry about you if you did, Raleigh," she said, as sensibly as her trembling voice would allow.

"My hair's started turning gray," he said, bouncing his fingertips off his temples. "I can't read without my glasses. What the hell was I thinking kissing someone almost ten years younger than me?"

She began to smile. He held up his hand and said, "Don't answer that. Listen, I apologize. This never should have happened. It was poor judgment on my part. I took advantage of—" She was laughing. He rolled his eyes. "You think this is funny?"

"Hysterical," she said, making unladylike sounds as he tried staring her down.

"This is simply a reaction to the embarrassing situation we're both in, but if you could try getting control of yourself…"

Pressing her lips tightly together, she pulled in air through her nose, then covered her mouth with her hands when she burst into laughter once again.

"Oh, Raleigh, you should see yourself. Standing there all outraged and sanctimonious when what I know, and you know, is that you enjoyed that every bit as much as I did." She managed a gulp of air before continuing. "So, do you want to tell me what really prompted this lecture?"

The honest tone of her reaction told him she had nothing to hide. Nothing to fear. Nothing to hold back. She was everything he wasn't, the opposite in every way that counted and, as incongruous as it might sound, those things made him want her all the more.

"Well?" she asked, drawing her brows together in a half-amused, half-impatient frown.

He looked out the window as bare branches clattered against the panes. How could he tell her, when he was afraid to face the truth himself—that it came back to his brother, Buddy? It always came back to Buddy; but this time was different. For the first time since his brother's death, he'd felt his heart touched by a free spirit. But unlike Buddy, she came wrapped in feminine charm, earthy sensuality and enough complications from their past to make him doubt his sanity.

Rubbing his forehead, he firmly reminded himself that after Buddy died he'd decided no one was ever again going to touch his heart so deeply.

"Rebecca, let's try to see this for what it was."

"And just what was it?" she asked, devilish humor making her eyes twinkle.

"A game we were both wrong to play," he said, as he studied her on the love seat. Her hair mussed by his own hands, her lips made pouty by his hungry kisses and her chin pinkened by his stubble. Somehow the top button of her sweater had come undone, or had he managed that, too? In any case, her sultry stare had locked on to his. And if he didn't stop looking at her, one curl of her finger and he'd come running.

She dragged her teeth over her bottom lip instead, leaving the tender flesh a ripe and glistening shade of crimson. He made a move in her direction, then stopped dead in his tracks. "Ah, hell, let's forget I ever came up here," he said, turning on his heel and heading toward the kitchen.

She followed him to the door, and when he turned to say goodbye, her winsome expression was as bogus as his request.

"Raleigh?"

Her voice was as sweet and seductive as a chocolate-covered strawberry. The expensive kind whose price everyone complained about but willingly paid. He leaned closer. The kind to savor, to nibble. All he had to do was slip an arm around her, press his lips to hers and taste her again.

"Yes?"

She stepped close enough to run her toes across the top of his shoe. "I'm not going to be able to put this visit out of my mind until I know one thing."

Parts of his body began to hum when she moistened her lips again. He knew that look in her eyes; she was setting him up, and for once, he had to admit, he didn't care to stop her. The truth was, he was powerless to stop her. She'd been working a spell on him since the moment he'd seen her standing naked in his swimming pool. "Go on," he said, drifting closer.

"Are you, or are you not," she asked, sliding her hand down her hip then patting her backside, "kicking my butt out of this place?"

His mouth went dry as he fixed his eyes on her hand and what it so casually played against. "Don't worry about it," he said, knowing he'd be doing enough worrying during the next month for both of them. Backing out onto the landing, he made himself look away. "You explained your need to be here, and I accept that."

"So it's all right with you that I stay?"

"Sure," he said, grasping the handrail.

She leaned her head against the door frame and gave him a little-girl-lost expression. "Because if you didn't want me to stay you'd have evicted me." She batted her lashes and laughed that "gotcha" laugh. "So you must really want me to stay."

"Rebecca, you're pushing your luck." He headed down the steps past her muddy sneakers.

"Oh, Raleigh?"

He didn't stop until he'd reached ground. Turning to look at her, he felt grateful beyond reason for the sixteen steps and chilly wind between them.

"About that guardian angel who's been watching over me?" She flicked the imaginary being from her shoulder, lifted her chin and brushed her hands together. "She's outta here."

"Why did you do that?" he asked, knowing this was going to be the longest month of his life.

"Why do I need a spoilsport like her around now that I have you?" she asked, giving him a smile and a tiny wave before stepping into her apartment and closing her door.

He stood at the bottom of the steps looking up at her door until he realized he was blinking snowflakes out of his eyes. Big, fluffy flakes. The kind that tantalized the child in everyone, promising lots of fun and lots of trouble. And this was just the beginning.

Rebecca set aside the reindeer stencil and paint-dampened sponge as images from last night with Raleigh rippled through her mind . . . and body once again. What was she thinking of when she teased him with kisses, then joined in the lusty free-for-all that followed? She couldn't remember ever being that forward with any man. Pressing a hand against one of her warming cheeks, she tried to make sense of her actions last night. And his.

One thing for sure, offering to decorate the windows of the Chocolate Chip Café wasn't keeping her mind off Raleigh as she'd hoped it would. Shivers of pleasure raced merrily through her body when she closed her eyes and pictured him inches from her. Squirming on the window seat cushion, she bit back a smile as she picked up a Santa Claus stencil. What was she complaining about? These little side trips through last night's memories were producing the most delightful sensations. Those long, thoughtful looks he'd delivered across the love seat, the excessive concern in his voice when he reacted to her high jinks at the river and that hungry, achy way he pulled her into his arms...and then across his lap, provided her with enough erotic energy to give her shivers an NC 17 rating.

But beyond his potent show of good old-fashioned lust, Raleigh had convinced her of something else. His protests and reasons to stop making love were too many and too emotional to be anywhere near the truth. She sighed. So what *was* the truth!

"There you go, zoning out on me again. What's with you today?" Megan asked as she cleared off a nearby table. "You didn't even giggle when I told you Mrs. Denunzio said Anita joined a convent and wouldn't be coming to the reunion."

Rebecca positioned the Santa stencil on the glass to the left of the prancing reindeer, then shook her head. "I'm not going to pretend with you, Meggie," she said, pulling the stencil away and slapping it against her thighs. "It's Raleigh Hanlon. He's driving me crazy."

"What?" Megan took the space next to her on the window seat. "But I thought something romantic was happening between you two."

"It *is* happening," Rebecca said, giving her friend a playful shake. "Except he refuses to...well, to go forward even though all the signs are there that he wants to."

"What's holding him back?"

"He insists he's too old for me. That he was my teacher. That his hair's turning gray."

"He actually used a few gray hairs as a reason not to...?"

Rebecca angled her head to one side. "Pathetic, isn't it?"

They both solemnly nodded, then broke into fits of girlish giggles. When they'd brought their outburst under control, Rebecca shrugged. "All kidding aside, I've been thinking..."

"Go on," Megan urged.

"Well, that his rejection might be more about me than about him."

"You? Oh, Reb, why would you say that?"

She laughed uneasily. "He *is* a history professor. He puts a lot of stock in the past. Maybe he's having a hard time dealing with the fact that no matter what I've done with my life, I'll always be the girl from the wrong side of the river."

"Now who's sounding pathetic?" Megan asked as she pushed up from the seat.

"You're right. That was dumb," she said, picking up the stencil and taping it in place. "What was I thinking? I've worked too hard and come too far to whine about the past. And Raleigh Hanlon's anything but shallow," she said, thinking about the depths of emotion he'd displayed last night. She twisted away from the window to look at her friend. "But I think he's hiding something, Megan."

"No time like the present for a little probing," Megan said, pointing out the window.

Electric sparks began congregating low in her belly when she turned to see Raleigh outside. Looking both ways, he repositioned his package and portfolio then started his dash across the plowed street toward the café. He had the stride and movements of a well-trained athlete, making his breath-stealing leap to clear the slushy gutter both masculine and graceful.

Megan peeked beneath the reindeer as a gust of wind caught Raleigh's tie, sending the ends flying up from his dark blue shirt to flap against his lapel.

"I never really noticed how handsome he is until you pointed it out to me, Reb. He reminds me of someone, but I don't know who exactly."

Rebecca turned to Megan. "Try Superman."

"Oh-h-h, you've got it bad, girl," Megan said as the bell over the door tinkled, signaling Raleigh's entry.

Rebecca turned her attention toward Raleigh, then openly studied him. And it's getting worse by the minute, Rebecca thought, as Megan headed back to the counter with a tray of espresso cups.

The wind had whipped Raleigh's hair into an artful disaster, added a ruddy glow to his handsome face and given his eyes an extra sparkle when he turned them her way. His surprised expression made her smile as she pointed to the big red nose on the lead reindeer. "This one's almost as cute as yours."

He looked around the café as he took a step closer to the window. "Were you warm enough up there last night?" he asked, his proper and change-the-subject tone altogether too ancient for his thirty-something years.

"Why, Raleigh Hanlon," she said in a soft, husky drawl meant for his ears only, "we both know there was heat to spare."

He gave her a look that said he wasn't going to bother pretending he didn't know what she was talking about. "I'm concerned about you, Rebecca."

"That's a start," she said, sending him an outrageously flirtatious look as she delicately dabbed excess paint from the sponge.

He took another step closer. "I want to make certain that you understand how things have to be between us. Are you okay with that?"

She gave him a secret smile, and when he started to return it she spoke. "I've stopped laughing, if that's what you mean."

"Rebecca," he said in an impatient whisper as he dropped his things on the cleared table, then took the last two steps to the window seat. Bracing his hand on the molding, he looked around, then leaned his face close to hers. "I thought I made myself perfectly clear last night on that matter. It wouldn't work."

She stroked the back of his tie with her clean hand.

"Are you sure about that?"

He swallowed. "Perfectly."

Rebecca wrapped her hand around his tie and tugged him an inch from her nose. The movement caught him off balance. His hand slipped from the molding and landed high on her thigh.

"Well, last night it felt to me like it was working...beautifully," she said, placing her other hand on top of his and giving it a squeeze. The smell of steaming espresso, the citrus edge to his after-shave and the crisp winter air clinging to his tweed jacket blended to make a unique and tempting scent she would forevermore associate with him.

"Oh, Raleigh," she whispered, watching his hazel eyes widen with astonishment, "you're absolutely adorable when I catch you off guard like this."

"You're going to be difficult, aren't you?" he asked, removing his hand from her leg and taking back his tie.

She winked. "Am I ever," she whispered with gusto.

He looked down at the red paint she'd accidentally smeared on his hand and gave a bewildered sigh as he backed away. Picking up his package and portfolio, he mumbled something that sounded like ". . . just the beginning," as he headed for the counter.

Rebecca boldly listened as he handed Megan one of his packages. "It's your tablecloth from my party. I had it dry-cleaned," he said, as his gaze strayed to the cake on the display stand and then to Rebecca.

"Were you pleased with the service?" Megan asked, glancing over at Rebecca. Rebecca mugged wildly at both of them.

"Miss Barnett did a fine job," he said, after he turned back to Megan.

"Great. Maybe I'll hire her again sometime," Megan said, as Raleigh pulled a paper napkin from a dispenser and wiped his paint-smeared hand. "Can I get you something?"

"Just coffee. I'll take it over there," he said, pointing to a table in the back corner, "after I wash this off."

As he disappeared down the side hall, Rebecca quickly gathered her stenciling supplies and headed behind the counter to rinse her hands. "Let me take that to him," she said, nodding toward the cup of coffee Megan was pouring.

Megan placed the cup on the counter then stepped out of the way. "I didn't know I'd be hiring you back so soon. By the way, he likes it black with raw sugar. Two packets," Megan whispered as he came out of the men's room and headed for the table in the corner.

When Rebecca lifted the domed cover off the cake stand and began to cut into the cake, Megan leaned close to her ear. "He didn't ask for cake."

"I know," she said, breathing in the scent of hazelnut liqueur, "but he's dying for a piece of this."

"Are you reading his mind now?"

"Almost. He's trying to show me that he can control his sensual side when he's around me." She carefully placed the slice on a plate, then loaded everything onto a serving tray. "But I can't allow that, can I?"

She left Megan laughing into a tea towel as she headed for the far corner of the room. He'd already put on his glasses and was studying a notebook when she arrived at his table.

"Your coffee," she said, as she began unloading the tray. "Your favorite cake. And some extra napkins just in case you need them." He glanced up as she touched the side of her mouth. "You know how messy some people get."

"I didn't order the cake."

"But you wanted it . . . bad. I saw it in your eyes."

He gave her a warning look over his reading glasses. "If you're looking for a tip—"

"A big one."

He drummed his fingers on the faux marble. "Don't tease the professor."

"Finally." Clenching her fist, she hit it on the table as she slid onto a chair next to him. "I just knew there was such a thing as Hanlon humor."

He opened his mouth to speak, but only shook his head as he ripped open both sugar packets and poured the beige crystals into the cup. Stirring his coffee, he looked nonchalantly around the room before he spoke. "I suppose I should be thankful that you didn't do this to me ten years ago."

Rebecca planted an elbow next to his coffee, dropped her chin in the palm of her hand and smiled when he finally looked at her again. "Good things come to those who wait, Professor," she said, dipping a finger in the frosting. She licked her finger then touched his lips to shush his coming response. "You told me that once a long time ago."

Taking off his glasses, he set them on the table then stared at her for a long time. His expression was as mysterious and unreadable as a newly discovered form of hieroglyphics. The only thing that didn't need deciphering was the wholehearted, undivided attention he was giving her.

"Professor Hanlon? Excuse me, sir." The polite voice barely rose above the buzz of conversations going on at the tables around them. Raleigh was the first to look away.

"Mr. Brannigan," he said, with more interest and energy than was necessary, "good evening."

"Good evening, sir. When you have a second, can I talk to you?"

Rebecca turned to face the man standing behind her. "Richie Brannigan, how are you?"

"Hi, Rebecca," he said, his gaze nervously darting between her and Raleigh. "I heard you were back in Follett River."

"For a while." She turned to Raleigh. "I used to baby-sit Richie. He lives down the block from my mother."

"He's my best student," Raleigh said. "Take a seat, Richie."

Rebecca stood up and offered him her chair. "I have to get back to what I was doing. Can I bring you a cup of coffee first? Something to eat?"

"No thanks, Reb," he said. "I—I need to talk to the professor."

During the next ten minutes, Rebecca kept watch on the corner table. The intensity in the boy's face was as touching as Raleigh's sincere interest in what he was saying. Several times during their conversation Raleigh reached to give the boy a reassuring pat. After Richie shook Raleigh's hand and left the café, Rebecca grabbed a pot of coffee and headed toward the table.

"Is everything okay with Richie?" she asked as she refilled his cup. "He looks as if the world's caving in on him."

Looking up from his daily schedule book, Raleigh appeared to consider whether or not he should answer her question. She set the coffeepot on the table and took the chair again.

"Don't give me that student-teacher confidentiality speech," she said, raking her fingers through her hair. "I used to change Richie's diapers. What's up?"

Raleigh gave a heavy sigh then tossed his pencil on the table. "Richie's the kind of student every teacher hopes for. He's gifted, highly motivated and he's serious. I give him a lot of credit, pulling himself out of a less-than-optimum situation as he has."

Some of us do that, she thought, as Raleigh continued.

"Anyway, his father refuses to give him the necessary financial information for processing his scholarship forms. He wants Richie to quit college and work in his body shop."

"The man's a selfish drunk, Raleigh. Always has been, always will be. What does Richie want you to do?"

"Help him plead his case to the scholarship committee," he said, rubbing his chin as he looked down at his notebook. "And I'm going to..."

"I hear a but in there somewhere."

"I agreed to talk at career night tomorrow at the high school," he said, tapping a square in his daily schedule book. "The time for the committee meeting overlaps my scheduled presentation there. I know I'll be late," he said, squinting with concentration.

"What about someone filling in with a shortened presentation until you arrive?" she asked, raising her brows. Like me? she thought.

He waved his hand then reached for the fork and cut into the cake. "There's not enough time to find someone now," he said, too distracted with his own thoughts to notice her overture. He shrugged. "Ordinarily I would say Richie's emergency situation automatically takes priority, but my niece, Penny, and her class are part of this school district. They're being bussed over from Daleville for career night. I promised Penny I'd be there," he said, forking a piece of cake into his mouth.

"I wouldn't worry too much about it," she said, smiling as he took a moment to savor the flavor. "Things have a way of falling into place when you least expect them to."

"Rebecca, I take these responsibilities seriously," he said. "Lately my niece has been badly in need of a father figure." He set his fork aside and took an extra breath as he looked toward the door. "Her father was my brother. He died before she was born."

"Megan told me. I'm sorry to hear that," she said. "Were you two close?"

"Yes," he said before focusing his eyes on her. When he spoke again he strained to make his voice all business. "Penny needs all the support I can give her. She's counting on me. And so is Richie," he said on the end of a sigh.

"You really do care about the future of those two kids, don't you?" Rebecca asked earnestly.

"I feel that way about all my students," he said, crossing his arms and resting them on the table's edge. He leaned in. "What? Did you think I didn't care about you when you were my student?"

"To be honest, I never really thought about it in that way. Most of the time I was thinking you were out to make my senior year a singularly miserable experience for me."

He gave her a sad smile that made her heart leap with unnameable emotion. "Is that how I made you feel?"

She thought long and hard before she answered him. Maybe now was the time to clear the air. "Yes, you did," she said, leaning toward him as she pressed her fingertips to her chest. "And I couldn't understand why you never let up. It was as if you had a vendetta to square against me personally. I know I was a handful, but I was never what you could call mean-spirited."

"You got me there," he said with a shake of his head and then a chuckle. "Of all the things I could say about you, you were never mean-spirited."

She sank back into her chair. "I am so glad to hear you say that," she said, as an almost giddy sense of relief washed over her. Slapping both palms to her chest, she laughed. "I feel as if I'm finally being vindicated."

"Did you see me as that much of an ogre?"

"Well, I would never have cast you as Mr. Chips," she said, picking a hazelnut from the top of the cake, then licking it clean of frosting. "I mean, I sorely needed guidance and discipline, that's for sure. But I also needed to be trusted and to be given the benefit of the doubt occasionally. You weren't too forthcoming in that area."

"I had no idea I'd affected you like this. I guess I spent so much time reprimanding you I failed to tell you just how intelligent I thought you were."

"I survived," she said, darting little glances at him. She wondered if he had any idea how much those words meant to her even now. Yes, especially now that she was seeing him in a whole new light. "All I meant to say is kids need space to make mistakes so they can learn and grow from them."

He smiled warmly. "Are you saying that because of Show-No-Mercy Hanlon, you didn't get to make enough mistakes?"

She laughed as she stood up and reached for the coffeepot. "Oh, no, I made plenty of those, anyway. You just weren't there to catch me every time," she said, popping the hazelnut into her mouth. As she headed back to the counter she thought she'd never heard anything more wonderful in her entire life than Raleigh's laughter.

Five

Raleigh pushed back the sleeve of his topcoat, checked his watch, then exhaled a hearty curse through clenched teeth. He was twenty minutes late for his career night presentation and only now arriving at the door, as fate would have it, to his old teaching classroom at Follett River High.

The other rooms he'd just hurried by were already through with presentations, a few were still in the question-and-answer phase, but most had broken into informal discussion groups. Their lively chatter poured into the hall. He imagined the scene behind the door in front of him; a room full of bored and antsy high school seniors, one of whom was his niece, wondering why they'd ever signed up for Professor Hanlon's talk.

His spirits were on a definite downward slide as he reached out for the doorknob. What could be gained by showing up now? Not much, besides a chance to reassure Penny that he hadn't forgotten her. At this point, Penny probably didn't care.

He took a step backward. What the hell was wrong with him? Why was he allowing himself to be plagued by these emotional and overwrought misgivings? It wasn't his fault that saving Richie Brannigan's college scholarship had taken so long. The scholarship review committee was supposed to help students, not make them feel uncomfortable about the state of their lives. He could certainly empathize with the students' predicament. Lately his own life felt as comfortable as scratchy tweed on bare skin.

Where had that little gem come from? Exhaling roughly, he shook his head to clear it. "Just get on with it, Hanlon," he muttered, as he pushed open the door to the overheated, chalk-scented room.

Charlie Reisling, his Wednesday evening basketball buddy, met him with a thumbs-up.

"Talk about surprises," Charlie whispered as a student asked a question about travel in western Africa.

"Surprises?" Raleigh asked, relieved that he wasn't delivering a long-winded apology to his friend.

"You're not known for gambling, Hanlon, but you were right on the mark sending in this substitute. She's got them in the palm of her hand."

"She does?" Raleigh whispered back, staring blankly at Charlie while he tried not to appear more confused than he was.

"When you called to say you might be late for this, you didn't mention she was coming in your place. Then she showed up fifteen minutes before the students. Totally prepared," he whispered, motioning for him to move into the room. "Just look at her, Raleigh," he continued, as he angled his head toward the front of the room. "Who would have thought Reb Barnett would turn out so well?"

He closed his eyes. If this was one of Rebecca's practical jokes, he was going to throw her out of the apartment so fast he wouldn't have time to listen to her laugh. Opening his eyes he turned them toward the front of the room while Charlie quietly told him how he hadn't recognized her at first. Raleigh nodded as he removed his coat. He wasn't about to tell Charlie how he'd renewed his acquaintance with Reb Barnett.

Rebecca was at the chalkboard in the midst of writing out and pronouncing a list of villages she'd visited in the Ivory Coast. If his life depended on it, Raleigh wouldn't have remembered one multisyllabic word she was saying. Forget the travel posters, carved masks and woven wall hangings she'd brought, his gaze had settled on the most striking visual there. Rebecca.

Her ultrafeminine, red jacket made a perfect contrast to her mouth-wateringly short, black skirt. He thought he could spend all evening waiting for a peek at her midriff, but as she turned to the board, his gaze took off over her curves on a joyride south to that tricky kick pleat in the back. His libido went into overdrive when his gaze dropped to her shapely legs encased in sheer, black stockings, and neatly finished off with her just-high-enough black leather pumps. As he attempted to retake the course at a more leisurely pace, she turned and caught his eyes with hers. The warmth in her slow, "gotcha!" smile radiated into his bones. Would there ever be a time he didn't feel a soft sock in the solar plexus when she gave him that smile?

"I see Professor Hanlon from Follett College has shown up after all," she said, placing her chalk in the tray. "I'll turn what time we have left over to him."

Charlie gave him a questioning stare. "What do you say?"

Raleigh sensed the group's reluctance to give up their speaker when two dozen more questioning stares landed on him. Their silence spoke volumes, all of which he agreed with. Folding his arms, he leaned against the wall of his old classroom.

"And risk causing a student riot?" He shook his head. "Please continue, Miss Barnett."

A rumble of approval rolled through the room. With a courteous nod worthy of any self-confident business-woman, Rebecca turned her attention back to the students. For the next ten minutes, Raleigh watched and listened and was as impressed as anyone there. Her sense of humor, breadth of experience and natural ease filled him with a strange kind of pride. He knew he'd had nothing to do with the polished professional she'd become, but he couldn't shake the peculiar feeling that he was somehow connected to her victory there tonight. As he struggled to understand the reason, he recognized his niece's voice asking the next question.

"What did you major in at college?" Penny asked.

Rebecca took a deep breath and held it as she stole a glance at Raleigh. For the first time since he'd walked in she bordered on appearing unsure of herself. He sent a curious squint her way, then decided he'd probably read her wrong. When she began to answer Penny's question, Rebecca sounded anything but unsure of herself.

"While I'm certainly encouraging everyone here to further his or her formal education, I'll be straight with you. I didn't go to college," she said, brushing back the casual spill of her bangs across her forehead. "I was fortunate enough, though, to figure out what I wanted to do before I even graduated high school. Since then

I've taken courses at a community college in Florida. And I've studied on my own," she said, easing her bottom against the edge of the teacher's desk. "But I will tell you this. Whatever you end up choosing for a career, the most important thing you can do to prepare yourself for it is to believe in yourself. The only person who can stand in the way of success is you."

When Raleigh could tear himself away from Rebecca and her simple wisdom, he looked at Penny. His niece was hanging on Rebecca's every word as if they were coming to her carved in stone. This was the first time in months Penny was showing interest in anything other than the latest music video. And that she'd asked a question concerning college renewed the possibility that she'd take him up on his offer to pay her tuition. Penny was all he had left of his beloved brother, and he had Rebecca Barnett to thank for the cautious hope reborn in his heart for the girl. He looked back to Rebecca as she looked up at the clock.

"I can take one more question."

Before any of the students could raise a hand, Raleigh spoke. "I have one," he said, as he unfolded his arms and took a step forward.

Rebecca's surprised expression was followed by a warm, inviting smile. "Go ahead."

"Tell us, Miss Barnett," he said, slipping his hands in his trouser pockets, "was there anything in your high school experience that directly influenced your decision to enter the travel industry?"

"Your class."

Surprised, he pulled his hand from his pocket and pointed a thumb at his own chest. "My class?"

"Uncle Raleigh's?" Penny asked, whipping her head around in his direction.

"That's right. Professor Hanlon was my history teacher here at Follett River High. And while I wasn't his best student, I have to say that he was the one to inspire my interest in faraway places."

"You never told me that," he said, forgetting for an instant that the entire class was now glued to their exchange.

Rebecca rolled a piece of chalk between her palms as the students looked at him and then back to her. "We had...other issues then."

"Well, well, class," Charlie Reisling said as he walked up the aisle toward Rebecca. "Amazing what one can learn at career night. Unfortunately we're out of time, but I want all of you to thank Miss Barnett for opening a fascinating window on the travel industry." Charlie began a round of applause, then followed it up with an announcement about the community tree-lighting ceremony immediately following Rebecca's talk.

As the students headed for the door, Raleigh's gaze only broke with Rebecca's when his niece made her way over to him.

"Uncle Raleigh, Miss Barnett has the most awesome stories. I didn't know she used to be your student."

Raleigh recognized hero worship when he saw it, and he wasn't going to pass up the opportunity to make it work to his advantage. "Maybe I can get you two together to talk more. Would you like that? Miss Barnett's staying in my garage apartment while she's in town."

"Oh, that would be...how did you used to say it back then?" She crossed her eyes, looped an arm around his and jiggled her head. "Bitchin'?"

"You'll never get me to admit that, young lady," he said as he managed to hold back his laughter. "Go on.

Your friends are waiting. And don't forget to say hello to your mother for me." Accepting a quick kiss on his cheek, he watched Penny leave as Charlie approached him.

"I think I'll herd these puppies over to the square," Charlie said, pointing to the students moving out into the hall. "Maybe you could see Rebecca to her car."

"No problem," he said, struggling to appear nonchalant as he waved Charlie out of the room. The door closed and suddenly he was alone with Rebecca. He slowly turned his head in her direction. More than a centerfold fantasy living on his property, she was funny and smart and obviously accomplished in her career. And when he thought how he'd been comparing her to Penny, he began feeling like a jerk. Next to Penny's teenage affectations, as endearing as they were, Rebecca presented a well-put-together package whose energy and sense of humor he would never again mistake for mere teenaged antics.

He started up the aisle toward her. She was bent over a desk, seemingly intent on rolling up her travel posters. But the closer he got, the deeper her dimple became until she surrendered it to a smile.

"I didn't know what to think when I walked in and saw you up here," he said, taking his other hand from his pocket to rub the back of his neck. "You never cease to amaze me."

Her lashes swept upward until her gaze was locked on his. "Is that a 'thank you, Miss Barnett'?"

"Yes. A big one, as you like to say," he said, picking up two rubber bands as she tapped the edges of the rolled posters against a desk. "Do you always travel with a collection of African masks?"

"They're Christmas presents for my family. I'll rewrap them later."

He nodded. "My niece was impressed with your presentation. Everyone was," he said, sliding the first thick elastic over one end.

"Were you?"

Glancing up at her, he matched her smile as he fumbled with the remaining rubber band. "Yes. What was that remark about my inspiring—?" His question broke off as the stretching elastic popped off his fingers, shot across the desk and hit the chalkboard.

"Next time I have a mind for classroom mischief, remind me not to put you in charge of water balloons," she said as he stepped behind the desk to retrieve the rubber band. Her easy laughter scattered his thoughts like snowflakes in a breeze.

"Speaking of classroom mischief," he said, joining her again, "I was standing back there remembering one of your more unforgettable escapades."

She squinted. "Which one?"

"Your Venus de Milo imitation," he said, thoroughly enjoying the memory as he slipped the band around the other end of the rolled posters. "I'd stepped out of the classroom and when I walked back in, there you were, standing on your chair with your black leather jacket tied around your hips and your arms bent back behind you."

She pondered his words as he helped her slip the posters into a cardboard tube. "Yes. I remember that now," she said, brushing back a lock of hair. "You asked me what I was doing up there and I said I was bringing life to dead art for a little extra credit."

"Right," he said, riveting his attention on the chestnut highlights in her hair. Her hairdo, a clever blending

of sexy sophistication and casual disarray, was a far cry
from the bleached blond, spiked one she'd worn ten
years ago. The way it freely moved around her face made
him want to sink his fingers into it and—

"Raleigh? I asked you a question."

"Sorry," he said, clearing his throat. "What was it
you asked?"

"Did I have all my clothes on?"

In the frantic seconds following her question, he
struggled to remember if she did. How could he, or she,
for that matter, possibly forget—? His shoulders suddenly and dramatically sagged as he swore under his
breath. She'd managed to pull his leg again, and with
resounding success. Like a reflex he lowered his chin and
shook his finger at her. "Miss Barnett!"

"Yes, Mr. Hanlon?" She bit down on her lip to stop
the sound of the laughter that was shaking her body.

Something fuzzy yet intense swelled in his chest when
the sound of her laughter broke free. She had a way,
when he let her, of making him feel young. Alive. And
needy. He pulled in a deep breath and waited for that
well-fought-for control to kick in. "Okay, okay, I get
it," he said, "there's one born every minute. Right?"

"Just teasing," she said, pretending to bounce a hit
off his chin.

His hand closed over hers before she could pull it
back. The smell of chalk and pencils drifted away, replaced by her fragrance. "Careful," he said, keeping his
tone playfully light, "I bruise easily."

"I'll remember that," she said, as he let go of her
hand. Without missing a beat, she continued, "Was
Richie Brannigan thrilled when you saved his scholarship?"

"The boy was close to tears..." He shook his head again. "Wait a minute. I just came from that meeting. How did you know?"

"Oh, I never doubted you'd take care of it," she said, as she began wrapping up the African masks and placing them in a box. "You see, where we differ is that I know what to expect from you."

"Am I *that* predictable?" he asked, helping her.

"That wasn't meant to be a kick to your ego. All I meant was that, when it comes to teaching, if you say something you usually mean it. Feel better?"

"Loads," he said dryly as the room lights blinked. "That's the five-minute signal before they lock up. We wouldn't want to be stuck here for the night."

She glanced around the room. "Oh, speaking from experience, it's not so bad," she said, with a mischievous grin.

"Do I want to hear about that?" he asked, picking up the rest of her things.

"So much, you can't wait to hear about it," she said, as she slipped on her coat and picked up the last box.

Following her down the aisle and out of the classroom, he pretended he couldn't have cared less if she told him. But that wasn't quite true. He was coming to enjoy these sojourns into their past. Viewed from a ten-year distance he could safely enjoy the thrill, knowing she'd survived it all. He stopped when they reached the outside door. "Okay. My classroom?"

She looked back, properly aghast. "You have to ask? Of course, it was your classroom."

"You're right. I can't wait to hear about this one," he said, pushing open the door and letting her pass. He walked her to her car as she recounted the harmless fun she'd had with her friends.

"So you see," she said, unlocking her car trunk, "it was a small party, no one found out, and we cleaned up afterward." She placed the box inside, then moved over to allow him to do the same as she continued, "We needed to blow off some steam because it was right after mid-terms. Even Jade Macleod was there that night."

"Jade?" he asked, trying to picture her, his star pupil, the class president and valedictorian, in on something questionable.

"Jade," she confirmed. "She worried the whole time that we'd be caught and something would go on her permanent record about it." Rebecca stopped and looked up wistfully into the clear, starry night. "I told her to consider it a necessary experience, a first and last time flirting with danger. And that when the night was behind her she could use it to gauge all the questionable situations to come." She reached into the trunk and pulled out her snow boots.

"And what did she say?" he asked, not wanting to let go of this crazy conversation, the way he was feeling and, most of all, this time with Rebecca.

"Hold on to me, will you?" she asked, wrapping her hand around his arm while she removed one of her pumps and tossed it in the trunk. "She said that was the biggest load of garbage I'd ever tried to dump on her, but, in the end, she managed to polish off two wine coolers and do the hula with Megan and me on your desk." She slapped him playfully on his shoulder. "Stop laughing or we're both going to fall."

In the divine struggle that followed, she managed to put on her boots and collide with every inch of him while she did it. Her thick coat might as well have been made of fragile silk because when she finally stepped away from him he could still feel the softness of her breasts pressing against his arm, and the almost rhythmic bumping of her hips against his. When she reached for the trunk, he stopped her. "I'll get that," he said, looking for some way to vent the energy she'd stoked in him. Making sure that everything was safely stowed, he asked, "Did you know you have a suitcase in here?"

"Oh, that. I'm taking the train to New York City tonight. This is all hush-hush, but I have meetings scheduled with a company interested in redeveloping the warehouse property plus a ton of Christmas shopping."

He felt the strangest sinking sensation throughout his body. She was going away. He shut the trunk. He wouldn't be seeing her for...how long? He scratched his head. "When are you getting back?" Keeping his back to her, he made sure that she didn't see him wince when he realized how he must have sounded.

"Saturday afternoon. Are you going to miss me?"

Much as I hate to admit it, yes, dammit, I am. And how this happened, I'll never know. He turned to her, and with a wary sigh, shoved his hands in his pockets. "Let's say, I'm getting used to having you around."

She winked. "You make it sound as if I'm a potentially dangerous situation," she said as they began walking up the street toward the town square.

Before he could shrug off her peculiar choice of words, she pointed up the street to the tall, floodlighted spruce and the activity going on around it. The streetlights were gleaming off her hair and face, making him think of anything but that she was potentially dangerous. Her face was aglow with genuine excitement. "One decorated tree in the town square, and they've turned this town into a Christmas card." She slowed to a complete stop, as the high school band wound its way through a discordant mix of notes from the wind section, one tortured xylophone and several tinny sounding drums.

As Raleigh looked at her a little longer he felt his heartbeat fall into step with the erratic sounds.

She scrunched up her shoulders and leaned one against a tree. "Wherever I am at Christmas, I always think about Follett River. And when the band gets its act together, I think I'm in an old-fashioned holiday musical."

A wave of nostalgia suddenly wrapped around his insides like a giant ribbon, knotting itself over his heart. "I'm taking your advice and putting up a tree. Next Saturday night. Maybe you'd like to help me decorate it?"

Her next breath came out of her nose in a steady, smokelike rush. "Raleigh Hanlon, are you trying to ask me out on a date without it sounding like one?"

One way or the other, the moment he answered her there would be no turning back. Carefully examining the inside of his teeth with his tongue, he realized he'd been putting off the inevitable. Of course, he could slow things down by telling her he was also inviting Penny so the two could talk. That would be the safest way to go. Wouldn't it? He looked at Rebecca, and all thoughts of safety fled. Her blue eyes widened with understandable impatience.

"*Tsk!* That was a tough question, wasn't it?" she asked, not bothering to hide her frustration.

Shaking her head, she started to walk away, when he took her by the arm and brought her around to face him. What the hell was wrong with him? He couldn't ignore this any longer or he'd need his head examined.

"Yes, I'm asking you out on a date," he said, and, as if on cue, the tree lights came on and the band dived into an energetic rendition of "Jingle Bells."

They both looked toward the tall spruce with the colored lights and shimmering ornaments. "With special effects, no less?" she teased, as they both began laughing. "Since you went to all that trouble, how could I possibly say no?"

Six

A shiver skated up Rebecca's spine when the snow-flakes outside the New York City office building began thickening before her eyes. She'd been happily counting down the minutes until her date with Raleigh, and that was the last thing she wanted to see. Shoving aside the image of it drifting across the train tracks back to Follett River, she took a deep breath, then regripped her suitcase and briefcase. Not that she believed in omens, but the sooner she arrived at the station, the calmer she'd feel.

By the time she'd made it curbside, the snow was blowing so hard she couldn't see to the decorated tree across the street. All around her, die-hard shoppers plodded along, their heads lowered against the gusty wind. Forcing a sympathetic, if apprehensive, smile onto the bottom half of her face, she swallowed uneasily. Thank heavens she'd finished that last-minute Christmas shopping yesterday; she wouldn't want to be sand-wiching in the task now. There wasn't a taxicab in sight.

Fifteen frustrating minutes later she pushed the hand of an irate businessman from the door handle of *her* hailed taxi. "I'm from Jersey. Don't even think about it," she warned, as she climbed in and slammed the door.

Ten minutes later her assertive move had inched her half a block up the street into snarled traffic before the taxi stopped moving. She checked her watch, then tapped it with her fingernail. This wasn't happening. Squirming in her seat, she alternately rubbed her brow and took deep breaths. What was she worrying about? Raleigh wasn't going to change his mind about their date if she arrived on a later train. Would he?

Reaching into her purse, she pulled out a bill and dropped it into the front seat. "Sorry, Ahmed," she said, after glancing at his license, "I've ridden hobbled donkeys that moved faster than this."

"It's coming down pretty hard," Ahmed said. "You sure you want to do this?"

"Do I ever. I've got a date tonight that I think I've been waiting for all my life, and if I have to hijack a snowplow and drive it to Jersey, I will." Grabbing up her suitcase and shopping bags, she headed into the street.

She got to the crowded station in plenty of time to wait another thirty-seven, nerve-wracking minutes for her delayed train to arrive. "Relax," she said to herself as she moved down the aisle of the car. There was no rea-son to be so tense; after all, she didn't believe in omens. Raleigh would be at the Follett River train station to pick her up, just as they agreed. Just then the train lurched into motion, throwing her into an empty seat.

But as her connecting train sped through the snowy New Jersey countryside, one doubt after another began creeping in. Nothing she could do would change the difference in their ages, their distinctly different backgrounds and his penchant for dwelling on both facts. What if Raleigh *had* changed his mind? What if he'd returned to thinking of her as the girl from the wrong side of the river? What if he was back to being Show-No-Mercy Hanlon? By the time the train jolted to a stop at the Follett River station, her patience was as frayed as a snapped ribbon.

"What if you get a grip, Reb?" she whispered impatiently as she rubbed clear a spot on the fogged up window. She'd never wasted time or thought on groundless speculation in her life and she wasn't starting now. If Raleigh promised he'd be there, she had no reason to doubt him.

Pressing her cheek against the cold glass, she strained for a glimpse of him. When she didn't see him, she angled her face in the opposite direction and searched the crowd again. He could be late. He could have had an emergency. He'd be arriving. Any moment.

"This is Follett River," the conductor said. "Weren't you getting off here, miss?"

She squinted furiously through the window one last time. *Come on, Raleigh. Even your shadow would do around now.*

"Miss?"

"Yes," she finally said. Gathering her bags, she headed toward the door at the front of the car. The shock of cold wind blowing up the train steps took her breath away and threatened to plunge her into the deepest pit of depression known to womankind. The one marked Extreme Caution: Man Trouble Ahead. She looked down and took the first step with a sigh. He'd changed his mind after all. He wasn't coming.

"Rebecca!"

The moment she saw Raleigh emerging from the opposite side of a baggage cart she would have sworn she heard trumpets. Christmas was coming early this year, she thought as she watched him making his way to her in those long, even strides she'd come to recognize as his. Her insides were tickling her in the most peculiar way as she consumed him with her eyes. His topcoat continued whipping against his trousers, his tie was playfully lifting and settling against his white shirt and his hair was ruffling against his forehead. Suddenly the doubts and discomforts of the last three hours were melting away.

"You look surprised to see me," he said, taking her suitcase and setting it on the platform. Helping her down the last step, he gave her gloved hand a gentle squeeze. "Did you think I wouldn't show?"

"Raleigh Hanlon," she said, her voice full of false bravado as her heart continued hammering at the sight of him. "I never doubted for a second that you'd be here."

She half expected a welcoming kiss, but when she followed his gaze toward a knot of students lingering on the platform, she knew she wasn't getting one. That was all right, she told herself. At the moment his sheer presence and broad smile were enough. And they had the whole night ahead of them.

As they walked to the parking lot, he asked all the appropriate questions about her meetings, the weather and the kind of train ride she'd had. The kind of questions one asked in public. The kind of questions one had to ask because the important ones were being saved for later... when they would be alone.

She smiled when she thought about the questions she would ask him. Intimate questions fit only for new lovers. She glanced up at him as their steps slowed to a stop by his car.

Raleigh leaned an elbow on the roof and smiled back at her. A long, knowing smile that said he'd missed her. A lot. And he was pleased she was back. Colored lights from the station's decorations were reflecting off his hair. She drew in a deep, dreamy breath and caught a whiff of his citrusy after-shave. He not only looked good enough to eat, he smelled that way, too. She reached to tuck his tie back inside his coat as he moved a step toward her. The moment glimmered with promise.

"Hi," she whispered.

"Hi," he whispered back.

With that smoldering look he was giving her, she half expected steam to rise from their bodies. Raising her chin, she parted her lips in anticipation of his kiss. *Now,* she wanted to say. *Kiss me now.*

He started down for her mouth but his momentum faltered when a noisy group stopped beside them. Instead of kissing her, he turned to shield her from their inquisitive looks while they slowly loaded into a minivan. As the group drove off, more people walked into the parking lot. He backed away from her completely, then reached in his pocket for his car keys.

"I made reservations at Boccaccio's," he said, unlocking the back door and placing her suitcase and shopping bags inside. "Hungry?"

"I am now."

"That's good to hear," he said, looking as if he pretended he believed her. Opening her door, he waited until she got inside before leaning down. "They're doing something special with venison tonight."

"I can hardly wait," she said, thinking about their time together after dinner. She stopped wondering if he was thinking about that, too, when she saw him smother a smile.

A minute later as he was settling himself behind the wheel, his knee accidentally collided with hers. The slight jarring sent a pleasurable rush of sensations up her thighs and into the already tingling center of her body.

"Sorry." He gently patted her knee then left his hand there a few seconds afterward.

"It's okay." The heck it was okay. It was wonderful. So wonderful she made herself close her hands over her arms to stop from reaching out and pulling him toward her like a love-crazed teenager. She coughed softly.

"I hear the waiters at Boccaccio's sing opera while they're serving you," she said, trying to keep her mind off the way he was removing his gloves and flexing his fingers. Her thoughts strayed back to the night in her sun porch when he'd wrapped them around her hips and pulled her down on his lap. She gave her head a quick shake and stared straight ahead at the snow-crusted windshield. Raleigh had been thoughtful enough to reserve a table at Follett River's finest gourmet restaurant for their dinner. The least she could do was pretend she was interested in eating it. But under no circumstances were they going to linger over the spumoni! "Is it true?" She looked over at him. "Do they sing opera?"

Raleigh leaned across the car's shadowy interior, slipped his fingers into her hair and drew her toward him for the kiss she thought would never come. His moves were slow and promising, tender and tantalizing and altogether worth the wait. He lifted his mouth from hers just enough to draw his thumb across her lips. "We'll just have to find out about that, won't we?"

"Yes, we will," she said, softly biting the pad of his thumb. Before she knew it, the teasing nip had turned into something hot and demanding. The car windows were already steaming over when she began inching toward him.

"I missed you," he said, reaching inside her coat to curve his hand over her hip.

The solid feel of his caress had her gasping from the deepening pleasure. "Me, too," she said, allowing her fingers to stray over the firm muscles of his chest as he kissed her again. Bold images filled her mind the longer she lingered over the masculine temptation of his hard body. If she didn't stop now, she'd be guiding his hands to the elastic on her panties . . . and beyond. "Raleigh." His name was all she could manage as she forced herself to stop kissing him and gently push him away.

"We should go," he said, leaning away from her.

"That's what I was thinking." But not what she was wanting. Licking a taste of him from her lips, she stole a glance at him, then muffled a sigh of disappointment. She wanted him. Now. Badly. She squeezed her eyes shut. So badly that she was considering making love in the front seat of a car for the first time in her life.

Taking another slow breath, she smoothed out her coat. She was crazy to even think about it. The scenario reeked of randy teenaged shenanigans. Leaning back against her door, Rebecca pressed her hands against her collarbone and laughed.

"What's so funny?" he asked, as if he wanted to find something to laugh about, too, in the awkward moment.

"I guess I'm surprised at how hungry I'm feeling."

He stared at her until he broke into a grin, then slipped the key in the ignition and started the car. "Hungry?

Rebecca, I'm starving over here." They were both laughing as he drove out of the lot.

By the time the venison was eaten and the arias sung, Raleigh was ready to grab Rebecca's hand and head for home. They'd exhausted polite conversations about his work week at the college, his former students expected at Rebecca's high school reunion and a dozen other subjects—and they all paled next to the subject at hand: the woman across the table from him and the longing he had for her. He'd been exchanging hot looks with her for the past forty-five minutes, and it was definitely time to be alone with her. As he turned to ask for the check, the waiter was rolling the dessert cart next to their table. Raleigh cast a doubtful look at the sumptuous display of spumoni, cannoli and tiramisu. Tonight was an excellent opportunity to bring his sweet tooth under control. He drummed his fingers on the table. Of course, Rebecca might want some. He let a cautious look stray her way, then felt his pulse quicken. She was checking her watch.

"Maybe we should get home to decorate the tree," he said, offering his hand to her across the white linen tablecloth.

"Tree? Oh, right. Decorating," she said, placing her hand in Raleigh's. They looked up at the waiter.

"Just the check," they both said on the same breath.

Thirty minutes and another aria from *La Bohème* later, Rebecca was wriggling out of her coat in Raleigh's foyer as he was tossing his on the floor. Before hers landed next to his, he was pressing her back against the door and trailing kisses across her jaw. She clutched at his arms, then began kneading the hard swells of biceps.

"Raleigh," she said breathlessly, as she twisted her neck to accept the full impact of his kisses. "I'd have died if I had to sit there and watch you eat dessert tonight."

He lifted his face and smiled. "Miss Barnett," he said, stroking her cheek with one finger. "I still intend to have dessert tonight. I just thought it would save us more time if I brought it home with me."

Her forehead wrinkled as she looked past his shoulder. "You did?" she asked, a second before she realized he was talking about her.

As she laughed against his shoulder, the vibration of her body enticed him closer. There was a fundamental joy about the feminine feel and sound of her that reached deep down where his old guilts lay in wait. Old guilts that had no place in his life tonight, he reminded himself. "Rebecca, this is the craziest thing I've ever done. All those years ago, I never imagined anything like this."

"I'm so glad you said that," she said, with an endearing intensity that touched him still deeper. "Because I feel the same way." She smiled her hand over his backside, then pulled him close, pressing his arousal against the flat plane of her belly. "Raleigh," she whispered, offering her parted lips to his, when someone knocked on the door.

They both froze in the surreal moment as if they'd suddenly been slammed back to earth by the sound. Raleigh swallowed hard, touched a finger first to his lips and then to hers. "Maybe they'll go away," he whispered. The knock came again.

"Maybe reindeer know how to fly," she whispered back.

"Uncle Raleigh? Are you in there?"

Raleigh let his shoulders droop as he stepped back from Rebecca and shrugged. Taking a deep breath, he retucked his shirt then helped Rebecca hang their coats on the coat tree. He told himself he'd waited this long for Rebecca and a few more minutes wouldn't kill him, but his aching body wasn't buying it.

"Penny?" he called out, as the girl began leaning on the doorbell. "Is that you?"

"Jeese, of course it's me. How many people call you Uncle Raleigh?"

"Only the lucky ones," he said jokingly as he glanced back at Rebecca to make sure she was ready. Then he opened the door and let her in. "What are you doing out this late on a school night?"

"Jennifer and I drove over so she could see her boy-friend," she explained, walking past him into the foyer. "Celia says—"

"That's mom to you."

"Mom says it's okay. I left a message on your answering machine. Didn't you get it?" she asked. "Oh, hi, Miss Barnett. Anyway, I told Jennifer she could pick me up here when she's through." Penny looked from one to the other as she took off her coat. "It's okay, right? You're not busy, are you?"

"Busy? Uh, well—"

"Actually, you came by at exactly the right time," Rebecca said as she took Penny's coat and scarf. "I promised your uncle I'd help decorate his Christmas tree and we were just about to start."

"Are you joking?" She looked at her uncle. "I don't remember you having a Christmas tree since before you and Karen were divorced."

"Then it's about time," he said, dropping an arm over Penny's shoulders while he gave Rebecca a look that he hoped she would translate as *later, I promise.* "Come on. I put the lights on earlier today."

"This'll work out great," Penny said, looking at Rebecca. "Now I can ask you more stuff about your job."

Between decorating the tree and listening to Rebecca's travel adventures, Raleigh had almost stopped thinking about making love to her. Almost, he reminded himself as he walked back into the library with a bowl of pretzels and soft drinks. He stopped to watch as Rebecca carefully hung a candy cane on a prickly branch. Her delicate but sure handling had him envisioning her fingers on him. As Penny chattered on about how cool Rebecca's stories were, Raleigh's stare drifted up from Rebecca's fingers to her eyes. From the twinkling look she was giving him, he had no doubt that she was reading his lusty thoughts.

"Are you doubting that last story I told?" she asked, her mischievous grin daring him to play along with her in innocent conversation.

"I shouldn't doubt anything you tell me anymore. But I'm still not sure if I believed you, during your talk at the high school, when you said I inspired your interest in faraway places. But that doesn't matter because I think you've been inspiring my niece. I've never seen her this interested in anything beyond high school."

"Uncle Raleigh, I'm definitely interested."

"Is that so?" Raleigh asked as he winked at Rebecca.

Penny peeled back the cellophane on the candy cane she was holding and snapped off the tip. "Really," she said, putting the piece in her mouth. "Listening to Rebecca has inspired me to start thinking about my future. At least I know the first thing I'm not going to do after I graduate."

"And what's that?" he asked, reaching up to hang a fragile glass ball on the tree.

"Well, I'm not going to college."

Rebecca watched the ball drop from Raleigh's finger-tips then slide off the tip of a branch before making a popping sound as it shattered on the floor. Ignoring the fine glass shards, Raleigh turned around to face his niece. Several heartbeats thudded in Rebecca's chest before he spoke.

"What did you say?" he asked, his grin still plastered to his face.

"I said I'm not going to college. Rebecca didn't go and look how great her life turned out."

Raleigh's grin collapsed on itself. "Penny," he said, on a controlled note. "I think we have to discuss this a little more before you can make that kind of decision."

"No, we don't, Uncle Raleigh. I've made up my mind."

The sound of crunching glass filled the room as he took a step forward. "Penny—" he began, his voice edgier this time.

"I'm not going," she said, lifting her chin in that way her uncle did when he wasn't giving in.

A muscle twitched along Raleigh's jaw. "I don't think your father would have approved of this decision."

"You can't make me go," Penny said, shaking her head as she crossed her arms. "Neither can Mom. And my father's dead."

Outside a car horn honked twice, and Penny's determined expression mercurially changed to a smile. Standing on tiptoe, she wrapped an arm around Raleigh's neck and gave him a smacking kiss. "Jen's here," she said, as if she hadn't just blown up his world.

She looked at Rebecca. "I can't believe you actually survived living in this boring little town. It's almost as bad as Daleville."

The car horn honked again, and she was headed out of the library before Rebecca could respond.

Swearing under his breath, Raleigh followed her into the hall where she grabbed her things. "We're not done talking about this," he said, as she shut the front door behind her.

In a few moments Raleigh appeared in the library doorway, his face a blank mask.

"Oh, to be that age again," Rebecca said with a comical shiver, as she knelt down to clean up the scattered shards.

For a long moment Raleigh stood in the doorway, his shoulders squared, his fists shoved deep in his pockets. When he spoke his low voice rumbled. "Didn't you realize how suggestible a girl Penny's age is?"

"Raleigh, this isn't over," she said confidently as she picked up the larger pieces of broken ornament. "Penny's young. I wouldn't be too upset."

"You wouldn't? Well, she's not your niece," he said, jerking his hands from his pockets and motioning emphatically with them as he began to pace. "You can afford the luxury of seeing a younger version of yourself on the edge of a big mistake. But I can't, Rebecca!"

"What's that supposed to mean?" she asked, feeling vaguely insulted by his tone, as well as his words.

"This . . . this path you've put her on is all wrong for her."

"Hey, I can understand why this latest thing doesn't go down well, but she's barely eighteen, Raleigh. Kids that age change their minds once a day on everything," she said, attempting to soothe him with a shrug and a smile. "Next week she could see a shivering squirrel outside her window and suddenly have a whim to be a veterinarian. Then it's off to college for her."

"Or she could talk to *you* again and decide she wants to postpone doing anything. You should have thought things out more before you spoke."

"Come on, Raleigh," she said, rising to her feet and placing the shards on a tabletop. "I'm not dumb. I know how much she means to you, but get a grip."

"Get a grip? This is serious," he said, striding over to the fireplace and slapping the mantel. "Time's running out to get her college applications in." Pressing his forearms along the edge of the mantel, he stared into the fire. "Are you suggesting I ignore that, too?"

Rebecca had never seen him this upset, even during one of her own teenaged escapades. But why shouldn't he be over the top about this? Penny was the only child of his dead brother, and he obviously felt a great deal of responsibility for her. The least she could do was let him know she understood his concern. She watched him for a second as he rubbed his brow while he continued staring into the flames.

"Of course, I don't expect you to ignore this," she said in a gentle, reasoning tone, "but she's an intelligent girl and this will pass. It did with me when I was her age." She opened her arms with a little laugh. "Hey, I turned out okay. Didn't I?"

When he continued staring at the fire, a cold, prickling sensation slid over her shoulders and down her back. Why wasn't he answering her? Didn't he agree that she'd found a direction and turned out fine after a less-than-glorious high school career? Didn't he see that she had made her life into something to be proud of? Didn't he know by now that she had grown into a responsible, respectable woman? She began to reach out to him. "Well, didn't I?"

"Look, give me a minute here," he said, continuing to stare into the fire as he gestured for her to stop. "This evening is turning into a disaster, and I don't want to say anything else that will make things worse."

As slaps in the face went, this was a stunner, but because it came from Raleigh, the blow to her ego nearly knocked her to her knees. With the sting of humiliation burning her cheeks, she pulled on the inner strength that had seen her through the worst. "For heaven's sake, Raleigh, don't let me stop you," she said in a whispery voice she hardly recognized as her own.

"What?" he asked, turning around to face her with a slightly dazed expression.

Raising her chin, she held the posture for a second, then nodded. "You want to know how you inspired my interest in faraway places? It was a moment just like this when I realized I had to get as far away from you as possible. You get your wish after all. I'll be packed up and out of the apartment by midnight."

Seven

"Rebecca, wait."

When she didn't, Raleigh followed her out of the library and down the hall to the door. "I'm sorry I took that out on you," he insisted, as she yanked her coat from the brass tree.

"Sorry's not good enough," she said, pushing him aside.

He stretched around her to take her coat, but she held it from his reach. "Rebecca, I don't want you to go, with things like this."

"It's always about what you want. About how you see things. About how you pass judgment. Ever since I came back to Follett River, I've been more than patient with all of it," she said, throwing her coat on the floor. "But that last remark was too much."

"Look, I apologize for whatever the hell I just said to make you this angry. But I swear I don't understand what's sending you over the edge. Talk to me." He watched her struggle to get herself under control. This wasn't Reb Barnett, the recalcitrant, obstinate teenager fuming over unfair detention. This was Rebecca, the woman, pushing all new buttons. "I'm listening now."

"You're faking."

"I'm not faking."

She looked at the door again, and he pressed a hand solidly against it.

Pursing her lips, she appeared to consider her options, then come rapidly to the conclusion that she had only one. To talk to him.

"I told you, despite my history, I thought I'd turned out okay. Then I asked if you agreed with me. And you said you didn't want to say anything else you'd regret. Just when I think I'm reaching you, you go all cold on me. You hold back!" She flattened her hand to her chest. "Raleigh, I'm not going to stay here and let you bash my character."

"I wasn't answering your question. I wasn't even listening to you."

Her eyes widened as she tossed her head and gave him a bitter laugh. "Oh, that's even better." Skirting around him, she made a grab for the doorknob.

Before she had a chance to touch the knob, he wrapped his hands around her wrists and pulled her against the length of him. "What's happening to us?" he whispered fiercely.

She turned her face away from his, but her soft curves remained tightly pressed against the hard planes of his body. The moment resonated with emotions that threatened to erupt with the first misplaced syllable he dared to utter.

Breathing in the scent of her hair, he told himself that if he kept on holding her close, her anger might melt into need. Anything was worth a try when he considered the alternative; her walking away from him. Shifting his stance, he felt her moving to push away from him.

"Rebecca, this is where we both wanted to be such a short time ago. Right here like this. Can't we talk this out?"

"I'm not sure *what* you want anymore," she said, looking back at him.

Their gazes locked and he suddenly understood that anger had little or nothing to do with the state she was in. Her eyes were shimmering with hard-held tears, and her parted lips were trembling with what he could only describe as shock and hurt.

"Come on," he said, sliding his hand into hers and leading her back to the library. He would have said her hand was shaking in his as they went down the hall, but the truth was it could have been his own. When he indicated the leather sofa in front of the fire, she eyed him suspiciously, then took a seat on the cushion farthest from him.

"I need you to understand something." *At least, as much as I can bear to tell you.* "Penny's my only link left to my brother. I thought I had pretty much convinced her to enter college next autumn. Tonight when she said she wasn't going, I felt as if I'd failed..." He closed his eyes. *Say it, you coward. Say you felt as if you'd failed Buddy all over again.* He opened his eyes but the words wouldn't come. "You were right when you said that I shouldn't expect her to know what she wants to do with her future, but her education is very important to me. It's something I've valued all my life. Once she has it, no one can take it away." He lowered himself on his haunches and rested his hands on her knees. "If I can't give her back her father, at least I'm giving her this opportunity. And if I can get her to accept it, I know she won't regret the experience."

The even line of Rebecca's lips and her downcast eyes would have dissuaded most men from continuing to plead their case, but he wasn't like most men. In the old days she'd still be ripping mad and plotting her revenge. But these weren't the old days.

"Rebecca," he said in the most reasoning voice he could muster, "name one person you know who passed up the opportunity of a college education and then didn't feel sorry about it afterward."

Licking nervously at her lips, Rebecca met his gaze. He sighed with relief; she was considering what he'd said. What had he expected? She was one of the most intuitive and understanding people he'd ever known. And because of that, the urge to tell her about Buddy and how he'd died too soon began clawing at his insides. He swallowed back the urge as he reminded himself that some things were better left to history. Besides, if he started down that road, he would lose it and turn into a blithering idiot.

"Anyway, I should be thanking you," he said, trying for a lighter tone and almost making it. "Since meeting you, she's beginning to show an interest in her future."

When Rebecca didn't respond, he moved to sit next to her on the sofa. Studying her profile in the flickering firelight, he quietly marveled at the proud way she held herself. From the lock of hair curving over her forehead to that gold bracelet glittering around her slim ankle, her rebel spirit glowed from every pore. A true original, Rebecca Barnett was the most intriguing, alluring and provocative woman he'd ever met. That he could be on the verge of losing her, shook him to his wing tips. Overcome with the need to make her understand, he began again, this time by whispering her name.

Rebecca pulled in a shallow breath and lowered her lashes at the sound of his voice. He was going to do it and there wasn't a thing she could do to stop him. With a sincere and compassionate tone that left her aching, he opened up her heart and took back the place she'd been holding for him there.

"I'm sorry I didn't make myself clearer that afternoon at Megan's café, but I want you to know now that I was always aware of your potential, your intelligence and that driving need to do something with your life." He hesitated, then looked toward the fire. "Buddy was a lot like you." He cleared his throat noisily then looked back at her. "To see that you brought it all together impresses the hell out of me. And if my niece does half as well with her life as you have with yours, I'll be genuinely happy. Believe me, you've turned out more than okay." Cupping her chin in his hand, he moved to press a kiss to her forehead.

Turning away, she made his kiss slide to her temple. "Please don't be kind to me. I'm the one who should be apologizing here."

"What for? No matter how upset I was about Penny, I shouldn't have taken it out on you. I deserved everything you gave me out there in the hall."

"Not all of it. And not like that," she said, touching her temple where the slight pressure of his kiss remained. She looked up at him. He was watching and waiting, his hazel eyes like two steady beacons guiding her past a rocky shore of memories. "You're a good man, Raleigh Hanlon. And now that I understand the reason you feel so responsible for Penny—"

"What do you mean by 'the reason'?"

"It's so clear to me now. I don't know why I didn't grasp the significance of it before. You loved your brother very much. When he died, you took on the role of surrogate father to his daughter."

Raleigh took in a shallow breath then let it out on a sigh. After all these years, he was obviously still grieving for his brother. Her heart ached for him, but she knew instinctively that he didn't want a maudlin scene.

Reaching out, she covered his hand with hers. "Raleigh, what I did was stir up an already difficult situation for you. And then while you were trying to figure out your next move, I took first prize for shallowest person on the planet by demanding you stroke my ego."

He started to shake his head, but she held up her hand and continued. "I can stand on my little soap box and stomp my foot all I like about how I succeeded without a college education, but that doesn't alter the fact that I feel as if I've missed something important by not having one."

"You don't have to say that because I'm Professor Hanlon," he said, as he loosened his tie and undid the top button on his shirt.

"I do because it's the truth. And I need to say this to...well, not just to someone, but to you." She gave him a halfhearted smile as he leaned forward to rest his forearms on his knees. "You see, you hit a raw nerve I thought had healed. What's that old saying? 'It's not the things you do in life you end up regretting, it's the things you don't do.' Well, as lackluster as my high school grades were, I somehow did well on my college boards. Raleigh, I had a chance to go to college and I passed it up."

"Rebecca—"

"I know what you're going to say. That I'm bright. That I've proven myself. That my life and work experiences have been an education in themselves, but it's not the same. At least, not for me." Shoving her fingers through her hair, she held on and gave an embarrassed shrug. "Look, this was not easy to admit, so please don't start lecturing me."

A century seemed to pass before she felt his weight shifting on the sofa. Lacing his fingers through hers, he lowered her hand then turned her face toward his. "I won't."

The world stood still with his warm and vital touch. Like a winter rainbow, the colored lights began twinkling on the partially decorated tree. The crackling flames in the fireplace were sending out the sweet, pungent scent of wood smoke. And from down the street came the faint sound of carolers singing a children's Christmas song. But more than any of those sensory suggestions, it was Raleigh's understanding look that began tempting her to believe the magic was back and building.

"But you want to," she said, holding on to her doubt as if it were the last rowboat, and a leaky one at that, in a vast sea.

He shook his head with hypnotizing slowness as he trailed his fingers down her chin and over the tiny buttons of her sweater. "No, I don't."

"Why not?"

He undid the first and then the second button. "Because I can't talk and kiss you at the same time," he said, curving his hands around her shoulders and pressing her back against the rolled arm of the sofa. "Rebecca Barnett, you amaze me."

"Wait," she said, holding her hands between them in a last act of self-doubt. "This isn't going to be one of those pity kisses, is it?"

He took her hands away and held them back on either side of her head. Trapped in his tender grip, she decided the masculine move surpassed any erotic moment she could have fantasized. No one had ever made her feel more desirable than Raleigh did. When his scorching gaze traveled to her cashmere-covered breasts, she instinctively pressed her hips against his. The undeniable evidence of his arousal pressed back, hard and heavy against her thigh.

"Does that feel like the beginning of a pity kiss?" he asked, beckoning her with a hungry look that tugged at her heart then sent it soaring. A wave of desire threatened to burn the breath from her body, but when she parted her lips it wasn't from want of air.

Bringing his face close to hers, he laid on a kiss to die for. He worked her mouth with his own, brushing his lips against hers then gently probing the moistness beyond with the teasing tip of his tongue. She made a whimpering sound in the back of her throat, surprising herself—and prompting him to further exploration.

Deepening the kiss to the recesses of her mouth, he stroked her with his tongue, telling her without words of the intimate act to come. And she listened to his message with every quivering fiber of her body. But when she began to respond with a swirling foray of her own tongue, he lifted his mouth and gazed down at her.

"Why did you stop?" she asked, as if she'd forgotten how to breathe on her own.

He let go of her wrists and, smiling, reached for another of her buttons. "Because unless you want to end up on the rug here in my library, we're going to have to think about going upstairs to my bedroom." Peeling back the edges of her sweater, he exposed the voluptuous curves of her naked breasts. "Soon," he said, then swore under his breath as he glided his fingers between the pale swells. "Very soon."

The last thing she wanted to think about was stopping what was already well under way. But he'd managed to resurrect one last smidgeon of doubt that demanded her attention. Unsuccessfully ignoring the gathering heat between her legs, she raised up on her elbows to glance around at the room that had been so intimidating a few weeks earlier. Skimming her gaze over the book-lined shelves and framed degrees, she quickly realized they were all a part of the package that was Raleigh. And any part of Raleigh's package was all right with her.

"What do you think? Shall we go up?" he asked, jutting his chin toward the staircase in the hallway.

While she weighed the decision, he lowered his head to lavish wet and warm attention on the sensitive tip of first one breast and then the other. The streams of pleasure tumbling through her threatened to paralyze her vocal cords.

"All those steps?" she asked when he stopped and she could catch her breath. "I don't think so," she said, as she unknotted his tie and with one tug, whipped the burgundy silk from beneath his collar, then tossed it over her shoulder. "Right here feels fine." Through a flurry of kisses, she managed to move off the sofa and settle on her knees in front of him.

Raleigh cupped her face in his hands and traced her lips with one thumb. "Good because I'd never have made it upstairs."

Moving between his thighs she lightly grazed his thumb with her teeth. "And I'd have never let you go."

Looking up into his eyes, she expected and found growing passion there, but as she waded further into their hazel depths, her heart doubled its beat. An ancient, untamed longing in his eyes was calling out to the deepest, most intimate part of her. The message was frank and to the point; passion like this demanded to be taken to the limit. Trembling with anticipation, she stroked the steel-hard muscles of his thighs. Everything she knew about loving and giving was about to change.

"I've waited so long for you," she said, realizing she was more than ready to go the distance with him. Wherever that might lead.

She lowered her mouth to the top of his thigh and bit him tenderly. When she heard him suck in a breath between his teeth, she lifted her mouth and smoothed the moist spot with her cheek. She was discovering that, like herself, there was something a little wild and needy and slightly dangerous in Raleigh Hanlon, and she wanted to experience the full power of it.

Gliding her fingers upward over the solid heat of his thighs, she pressed her thumbs against his hips then moved her cheek against the flat plane of his stomach. The moment resonated with pent-up perfection. Then he wound his fingers into her hair and lifted her head.

As his searching gaze circled her face, she drew her hand down his body until the distinct ridge of his arousal was pressing against her palm. "Raleigh?"

He encouraged her boldness with a scorching kiss, then took her in his arms and stood up with her. "Say it. I want to hear you say it."

"Make love to me . . . like there's no tomorrow."

"I plan to," he said, peeling off her sweater then kissing her again. Stepping back, he pitched the black cashmere over his shoulder and stared again at her breasts.

She'd never felt so vulnerable yet so safe. Whatever he had in mind, she was ready for. Eager.

His gaze traveled lazily up to her mouth and hair and then her eyes. The blatantly sexual stare delivered his masculine challenge before his words did. "But you'd better know that I have no intention of stopping, so if you're thinking about changing your mind say something."

She had no doubt that he meant every luscious, promising word he said. And the thought of him overcome with desire as he moved inside her spurred her to shameless action. "I thought I'd never hear you say that," she said, reaching for his shirt and tugging it from his waistband. In her haste she popped off the two remaining buttons as she pulled it open.

He held still, watching her as she circled him to strip off the material. When she saw what she'd uncovered she pulled in a slow, steadying breath. She expected an attractive body but nothing quite like this. Broad, straight shoulders, perfectly detailed muscles along his arms and back and a narrow waist that tapered smoothly into the waistband of his trousers. Trailing her hands over his arms then around to his front, she ran her fingers greedily through the thick mat of hair covering the sculpted muscles of his chest.

"Raleigh," she whispered between the wet kisses she began pressing to his chest, "you're so beautiful you make me forget to breathe."

Rebecca's sexy touch and hot mouth were threatening his sanity, but he had a hunch she wouldn't care if he lost his mind with her tonight. Each time she looked at him or touched him, he wanted her in every way a man could want a woman. Sinking his fingers into her hair, he lifted her face from his chest. "I'd like that pleasure, too, if you don't mind." Before she could respond, he lowered his face to suckle her breast. The sweet, clean flavor of her nipple filled him with an unknown yearning. He didn't try to understand it. Knowing that the longing had to do with her was good enough for now.

He could have gone on indulging himself, but her ragged moans prompted him to stop. "Too much?"

She shook her head. "It just feels so good," she said, gripping his shoulders. A lesser woman would have left it at that. But not Rebecca. "Do it again."

Lowering his head to her other breast he gently tested the taut, dusky bud. Quivering resistance made his mouth tingle for deeper contact, but she was soon pleading for him to stop again. And then to start. Instead he trailed a string of kisses up her neck until he was rimming her ear with his lips and tongue. Shallow responses were never her style. She began writhing in his arms as if she could seal her naked breasts to his chest.

"Raleigh," she said, pulling back and giving him a smile wicked and hot enough to melt snow. "You're making me crazy...wanting..."

"Wanting what?" he asked, biting back a playful smile.

She moved away and began unzipping her skirt while she toed off her shoes. With tantalizing slowness, she took down the skirt and then started peeling away what little feminine scraps of clothing were left. Down to nothing but her thigh-high stockings she moved her fingertips over their lacy tops in the most suggestive way he could have imagined.

"You know exactly what I'm wanting," she said moving a step closer. "And how I'm wanting it, because you're wanting it that way, too. This thing between us, you've known all along it wasn't going to be about kisses and tickles."

As he looked at the flickering amber light playing across her body, the realization struck him that he had finally found a woman who understood the passion in his soul. Passion that he'd tried covering with quiet anger and hard work and a dozen other substitutes over the years. Passion he had no intention of denying tonight with Rebecca naked, waiting and smiling that knowing smile a few steps away.

Without breaking their connected gazes he picked up two throw pillows from the sofa and tossed them on the rug in front of the fireplace. "You're so right. Kisses and tickles wouldn't begin to touch it." Reaching into his pocket he drew out a strip of three condom packets and dropped them on the sofa as he smiled back. "I just didn't want to overwhelm you."

Picking up the strip, she refolded it and tucked it in the top of one stocking while she looked him over with unabashed interest. "I dare you to try, Professor," she said, turning away from him with a little laugh to lower herself onto the rug before the fireplace. Stretching out on her side, she wrapped a hand around the pillow in front of her as she propped up her elbow to rest her head in the other.

As he stripped off the rest of his clothes, he couldn't take his eyes from her sleek curves outlined in the quivering light. In front of the flickering fire her provocative pose resembled a classic work of erotic art, right down to the fine gold ankle chain glinting through her stocking. The sight of it sent a distinct jolt of possessiveness through him. He wanted to know who gave it to her. And what that person had meant and might still mean to her. He wanted to know soon. But he had more pressing needs on his mind at the moment.

Kneeling behind her, he skimmed a knuckle down her spine, then ran a slow hand over her backside. Lowering his head, he nibbled softly on the lush curve until she closed her eyes and sighed. He moved toward her legs and, as she turned her head to watch him, he began peeling off one stocking.

"I like it when you touch me there," she whispered over her shoulder as she turned onto her stomach.

He swallowed hard. It was no use pretending; he couldn't experience the richness of her erotic nature without dealing with his own.

"Here?" he asked before delivering a soft, biting kiss to her buttock.

Pushing up on her forearms, she held back a gasp. "Yes."

He looped an arm around her and brought her back against him as he gave her buttock a gentle squeeze. "Like that?"

"Like that," she said, reaching to smooth her fingers over his hair-roughened thigh.

Her sensual moves and stunning frankness demanded more daring action. Skimming his hand over the juncture of her thighs, he parted her legs and slipped a finger into her slick heat. In return, she gave him the deepest, most luxurious sigh he'd ever heard as she squirmed between his finessing hand and the solid heat of his arousal.

"Since that night...on the sun porch...I've, oh-h-h...I've wanted to feel you like this."

"Like what?" he murmured.

"Moving against me," she said, "so hot and hard." Her titillating words had him growling softly against her neck. He'd had a wife for six years and a number of lovers, but none of them could reach down inside him and stir him this way. Other than Rebecca, he doubted if anyone could.

"When did you know?" she demanded as she moved her shoulders restlessly against his chest.

He didn't have to ask her to explain; he knew exactly what she meant. "I wanted you wet and whimpering like this that first day I saw you standing in my pool." He heard her breath catch as he probed deeper. "I knew I'd never seen anyone more beautiful, more desirable." He brought his mouth closer to her ear. "I wanted to touch you then so badly. Touch what I couldn't see. Touch what you wanted me to touch. Like this," he said, continuing to explore her tight channel while he reached up to roll one of her nipples between his thumb and finger. He felt her body tensing as he increased the rhythm of his strokes.

"Raleigh." She held her breath as she turned her face toward his.

"That's it," he whispered, watching the exquisite neediness in her expression. Her flushed cheeks, her parted lips, her half-closed eyes riveted to his, it was all for him now. And so was her holding back. "Yes, go ahead."

She could barely form his name on her lips.

He stroked faster. "I want you to. Like this. For me."

As she rocked against his hand, her little cries of surrender dug into his heart. Her stunningly realized climax nearly sent him over the edge with her, but he somehow held on. "Beautiful, so beautiful," he continued murmuring against her neck until her last shudder of ecstasy. When he heard her deep sigh of satisfaction it was as dear to him as what came before it.

Cries and moans or one long, soft sigh, it didn't matter. She was a precious mix of mother earth and moonbeams. He opened his arms as she nestled deeper into his embrace.

She leaned her head back to give him a long, wanton kiss. "I thought I'd died and gone to heaven."

"Tell me all about it," he said, running his hand down the flat plane of her belly to the damp nest of curls between her thighs.

She pulled the condom packets from the top of her stocking, ripped one from the strip and tore it open. "I've got a much better idea. Why don't you come with me this time," she said, handing him the contents.

While he rolled on the condom, she slipped off her stocking. "I thought you'd never ask," he said, taking her back on the pillow. Sliding down between her legs, he kissed her tender, feminine flesh until her light laughter became a troubled moan.

"Not that way," she begged, but he was already moving up and over her.

"This way?" he asked, skimming the tip of his arousal against her moist, satin folds.

"Yes, please, yes."

As if anticipating his powerful need for her, she opened to take him in fully and swiftly. Once inside her inviting heat, he held himself steady. He wanted to give her time to adjust to his size, but by the way she was moving he knew she wanted more from him than good manners.

There was no room for awkwardness, no place for timidity when she begged him to hurry. As if a dam had burst inside him, everything he'd been holding back poured into the pure passion of their union. They were oblivious to everything but their determined struggle, their whispered wishes and ragged cries filling the air. She was there with him every step of the way, sometimes leading, sometimes following and always exciting him more than any woman he'd ever known.

"Wait." She separated them, turned in his arms and enticed him to join her again as the wild struggle continued. He could hardly contain his happiness as he realized their desires were evenly matched and evenly met. When it was over, he held on to her, fervently hoping the joy he felt with her would go on. He needn't have worried. When he turned away from her to right himself, she ran her fingers through his hair then peppered his shoulders with kisses as if she still hadn't had enough of him.

"You make me feel so safe, so good . . . so wild."

He turned back to her, watching her with unveiled delight. "I believe," he said, giving her a teasing wink as he ran his finger down her nose, "we could be arrested in several states for a few of those wild moves."

"Really?" She hooked her leg over his hip. "That's so exciting."

The tree lights and glittering ornaments swirled past him in a glorious blur as she pushed him onto his back. Caging his hips with her thighs, she held him steady as she centered herself over him. "I haven't been arrested in years."

"Rebecca! What do you mean, you haven't— oh-h-h." He drew a hand over his face as he shook with laughter. "Never a dull moment."

She took his hand in hers and held it between her breasts. "Oh, Raleigh, who would have thought? Reb Barnett and Show-No-Mercy Hanlon enjoying each other so much. Laughing and talking and..." She shook her head. Her words drifted off as she lifted his arms to kiss them.

Watching her, he had the oddest mix of feelings. On one level, he was discovering her for the first time, and on another, he felt as if he'd known and needed her forever. Needed her? He looked away. He could understand wanting her, but needing her? He couldn't remember ever needing someone like this. And where did they go from here? Was there a future for them beyond this nearly insatiable hunger they shared for each other? There were so many questions he didn't know the answers to, so many he hadn't thought of yet. Glancing at her ankle, he managed a slight smile. Except the one that had intrigued his male ego since that day she stood next to him naked out by the pool. He looked up at her.

As if she'd read his mind, she smiled knowingly and said, "I'll answer one of yours if you answer one of mine."

"Okay," he said, deciding to let her scratch his itch. "Where'd you get the ankle bracelet?"

"My ankle bracelet?" she repeated, shrugging with surprise. "Jamaica. I bought it in Ocho Rios about a year ago..." As a smile began to grow on her face, she shook a finger at him. "You thought someone, maybe a lover, gave it to me, didn't you? Why, Raleigh Hanlon, I do believe you're jealous."

"Hey, I was curious," he said, tickling her until she made him stop.

"Look at me," she said, holding his face steady with her hands. "We haven't had much time to talk about other people. But now that this has happened, I want you to know that I haven't had a long string of lovers. I was with someone in Miami for about two years. We broke it off over a year ago.''

"Mind if I ask why?''

She sat up and crossed her hands over her breasts. "I've said it's because we grew apart, but I could never really put it into words. I doubt if he knew, either. He was a nice person. Generous. Thoughtful.'' She smiled. "Everything a mother could want for her daughter, but something was missing. Now I know what it was.''

A bomb could have exploded at that moment and he wouldn't have flinched. "What was it?''

"Passion," she said, taking her hands from her breasts to draw them down his body. "Passion and everything that comes with it. But you understand.''

He took both her hands and pressed his lips to first one and then the other. "Yes, I do. I was married to a lovely woman who tried for six years to... get to me. Rebecca, it's never been like this with anyone else.''

Holding her gaze to his in an act of silent communion, he watched her blue eyes warm and widen. He would have sworn she was glowing as she leaned down close to him. Her breasts brushed against his chest, calling back in him a desire to have her again.

"I can ask you anything, can't I?'' she whispered.

He nodded as the returning desire for her sharpened within him like a cracking whip.

She whispered her request against his ear, drawing out the exquisite details of her desire. He wouldn't have denied her anything, but he had to be certain about this. "Now?'' he asked. And then, "Are you sure?''

"Raleigh Hanlon, you have to ask? Don't you know by now that I'm planning to make your Christmas the merriest one ever?" Reaching for the condoms, she tore off another and dropped it on the center of his chest. "Even if it means getting arrested."

Eight

The depth of Raleigh's passion astounded her as well as inspired her. While she pleasured him with her lips and mouth, he wound his fingers through her hair and whispered words of such loving encouragement she thought the night must be a dream. But dreams could never be as rich, as vivid, as vital, as this loving act.

Soon he was stringing kisses and love bites over her body, insisting she take what she'd just given. And later when they'd momentarily exhausted themselves, she lay spooned against him because he insisted he didn't want to stop touching her. And because she couldn't think of another place she'd rather be than in his arms.

For the first time in her adult life, Rebecca felt complete. While he stroked her, she kissed his other hand as she stared dreamily at the lighted tree.

"You're awfully quiet for someone who was anything but, a few minutes ago," she said, as he continued caressing her body. "May I ask...?" She paused to control a shivery aftershock of pleasure. "What are you thinking about?"

"I thought you could read my mind," he said, his baritone voice vibrating against her body.

"I can," she said with exaggerated seriousness. "I'm just conducting a test."

He slid his hand over her hip and snuggled closer. "Well, I was thinking about us making love," he said, drawing circles along her waist with his thumb. "How you know what you like and don't mind asking for it. That you know what I like before I ask for it."

Smiling contentedly, she lifted his hand to brush his knuckles along her chin. Warm and safe within his embrace, their sensual awareness of each other continued to enchant her. Raleigh was right on target with what he'd said. Every wonderful kiss, every careful caress, every shuddering move they'd made together fulfilled a secret wish, a hidden desire, a deep need inside their hearts. "Raleigh," she barely whispered, just to hear his name on her lips.

"I'm not going anywhere." Stretching lazily against her, he nuzzled in the curve of her neck until she giggled. "I have another question for you."

"All right," she said, turning her face up toward his.

"Where did it come from?"

She narrowed her eyes. "Pardon?"

"This...this spirit that permeates everything you do?"

She thought for a moment, then laughed. With his hand still in hers, she pointed at the Christmas tree. "I think it started emerging under one of those about twenty-two years ago."

He pushed up on one arm and looked first at the tree and then, with healthy skepticism, at her. "That would make you, what, about six? Hey, do I want to hear this?"

"You can barely wait," she said, nudging him off balance and onto his back. "I grew up with two brothers and one sister in a very traditional family. The boys took karate lessons. We girls took tap dancing. They did yard work. We got stuck with the dishes. My sister never questioned it. I, of course, did."

"Of course."

"But I learned to live with it. Except for every Christmas when my heart was shattered," she said with an exaggerated frown, "because while Santa dumped all those unwanted nurses' kits and embroidery projects under the tree for me, he brought my brothers extra sections of track and new cars for their train set. Oh, and all those cute little bridges and tunnels and trees." Sitting up, she twisted around to face him. He was struggling to contain a smile. "And those adorable little cows and lamp posts and teeny tiny people to put in those perfect little houses."

"Life's unfair," Raleigh said, playing straight man.

"You're so right. I spent my precious minute on Santa's lap, for four years running, trying to explain why I needed my own train set. I told him quite clearly that my brothers refused to let me touch theirs. Stop laughing," she said, softly butting him in the chest with her elbow. "You can't imagine what it's like to have to sneak downstairs in the middle of the night and hijack a train set for a run around the track." Sitting back on her ankles, she shook her finger at him. "In the dark, mind you. Do you have any idea how incensed I was when my brothers caught me and— Raleigh, stop laughing," she said, breaking up into laughter herself. "Anyway, that was the defining circumstance for the rest of my life."

"And Santa never caved to your tale of woe?"

"Never." Reaching for his shirt, she slipped it on and flipped up the collar. Fluttering her lashes, she stood up and planted a fist against her hip. "Isn't that the worst tale of Santa neglect you've ever heard?"

"I can hardly keep from crying," he said, continuing to shake with laughter. "Where are you going?" He slid his fingers over the fine chain around her ankle. The casual caress filled her with unexpected emotion. The gesture was tinged with a kind of emotion that thrilled her. Whether he knew it or not, it said he'd staked his claim.

"With all this talk about Christmas, I just remembered I have something for your tree."

"For that you're taking my shirt and leaving me here alone?" he asked, unaware of the warm thrills scattering up her leg. Trailing his fingers over her foot and toes, he groaned theatrically when she began backing away. "Doesn't this constitute a form of neglect?"

"Hmm. You do look pretty lonely and naked over there," she said, continuing their lovers' nonsensical banter. He made her heart leap with one tantalizing grin when she bumped into the wall. "Oops. Think you can manage without me for about thirty seconds?"

"Thirty seconds?" Raising his hand, he turned it palm up and shrugged. "The least you could do is leave me something to remember you by."

"How's this?" she asked, flipping open his shirt to flash him her bare breast.

"I don't know. Let me see the other one," he said, with mock grumpiness. "Better yet, come back over here and let me do that."

"Thirty seconds, you impatient man. Then, if you don't like your present, I promise to crawl back on my hands and knees, begging your forgiveness."

She didn't miss his wily smile. "In that case, whatever you've brought, I hate it already."

"Shame on you, Professor."

True to her word, she was away for under half a minute. When she returned, Raleigh was zipping his trousers and walking over to the tree. "I didn't wrap it," she said, pushing rustling tissue paper aside as she picked a tree ornament out of the bag in her hand.

He took the sparkling apple by its gold cord, lifted it to his eye level and carefully twirled it around. Running his fingertip over the green glass leaves, he met her gaze over the apple. "Did you steal this?"

"Did I what?" she asked, knowing by his deadpan expression that he must be joking. She'd seen more sides of his humor in the last few hours than she'd ever seen when he was her high school teacher.

Shrugging grandly, he moved a candy cane from one of the branches and replaced it with the red sequined ornament, "I was hoping something was wrong with it. That way I could watch you crawling back across the rug on your hands and knees—ouch!"

"Raleigh Hanlon, what a terrible thing to say," she said, before tossing the bag on the floor and pointing at him. "Obviously that misdemeanor I was accused of in the high school cafeteria didn't make it onto my permanent school record, or you'd know a remark like that could traumatize me."

"Misdemeanor?" he asked, as he swept her off her feet and into his arms.

"Oh, no. What are you going to do? Turn me in to the cafeteria police for that incident?"

"Of course not. The statute of limitations has probably run out. Besides, I'm only involving myself in your criminal activities that include me."

"What a guy," she said as the Christmas tree disappeared, eclipsed from her view by his shoulder. "Where are you taking me?"

"Upstairs to my bedroom," he said, heading into the hall with her. "I have a few presents for you, too."

"But it won't be Christmas for another week," she said, smoothing her hand along his chest and over his biceps as he went up the stairs with her.

"Well, you can consider these pre-Christmas presents. And, unlike yours, mine are wrapped. I believe the package says hermetically sealed."

She thought for a moment then buried her face in his shoulder and laughed when she realized he was probably talking about more condoms. "I can't wait to open them. How many?"

"A lot. And wait until you see my personalized delivery system," he said, as he reached the second-floor landing.

She was laughing again as he pushed his bedroom door open with his foot. "You see, Miss Barnett, I intend to make your Christmas a very merry one, too."

For the first time in years Raleigh was identifying with his students. Although he found himself laughing freely at their jokes, even those directed at him, he was as eager as they were for the semester to end and the winter break to begin. Sneaking looks at his office clock became his new pastime. Time spent away from Rebecca dragged, so the sooner he could lock up his campus office and head home to her, the happier he was.

When she greeted him at his door in the afternoons, she was always spilling over with stories about her own busy day. During dinner she shared the latest news on her fast-approaching high school reunion, her visits across the river to her family and the continuing research on establishing her second travel office.

He'd been doing his best not to think about her leaving, so when she casually mentioned she would be spending a good amount of her time in Follett River once her office opened, he felt as if a weight had been lifted from his chest. He spoke more freely after that, telling her about his approach to teaching history and his long-held fascination with it. Halfway through explaining the book he was writing about pre-Columbian civilizations, he apologized for boring her. She insisted he continue.

By the specific questions she always asked, he became convinced that she was genuinely interested in what he had come to view as his rather mundane life. Maybe it wasn't so mundane after all. At least not since she had taken an interest in it and become a major part of it.

When Rebecca suggested that his daily phone calls to Penny might be hindering and not helping the high school senior to reconsider college, he stopped the calls. Her common-sense approach to dealing with Penny helped ease the frustration he felt about the girl's future. He opened, read and then found himself ignoring holiday party invitations because he wanted to spend more time with Rebecca. Then one afternoon that last week before Christmas she asked him out to one.

"Jade Macleod's family is surprising her with a 'welcome home' reception. You're bound to recognize a lot of people there."

"I'm sure I would," he said. Her excitement over the affair filled him with guilt about how much he'd been keeping her exclusively to himself. Then another thought struck him. The one party he couldn't ignore was being held the same night as Jade Macleod's. "Damn. I have this huge faculty thing that night. Even though it's going to be the same old same old, I can't miss it."

"Dean Callahan's party? That won't be a problem because—"

"Look," he said, cutting her off as he pulled her into his arms, "I've been very selfish with your time. Go on to Jade's party and have a ball. In the meantime I'll do my duty and go to that faculty thing."

"Raleigh," she said, playfully running her finger down his nose, "is this a way of telling me you're getting bored with me?"

"Absolutely not," he said, kissing her soundly. "But you deserve time with these friends, some of whom you haven't seen in ten years. Besides if you walk in with Show-No-Mercy Hanlon, they could all run shrieking from the place. No, I've been taking up far too much of your time." He pressed his fingers to her lips as he set her away from him. "It's no use. I'm going to have to insist you go to Jade's surprise party without me."

Hoisting herself up on a kitchen counter, Rebecca watched as he began searching through the refrigerator. She could tell him that she'd already decided what she was doing next Monday, but surprising him would be more fun. Smiling, she settled her shoulders against the cupboard doors while she admired the way his jeans pulled snugly across his backside. He'd been wearing jeans with his tweed jackets to the campus lately, and she couldn't agree more with his choice of wardrobe. If he were a few feet closer, she'd be hard-pressed not to deliver a well-placed pinch. "You're going to miss me Monday night."

"I will miss you," he said, standing up as he twisted the cap off a bottle of beer. Leaning an elbow on the door, he smiled, then took a healthy swig.

"More than you know," she said in a singsong voice as she picked out a tangerine from the fruit bowl next to her. She began tearing into its peel, sending a pungent citrus mist into the space between them.

"More than I know?" he asked suspiciously as he lowered the bottle. She watched his brow wrinkling.

"Yes. I promised I'd spend that night and part of the next day with my family. My mother's been complaining about not seeing enough of me."

"She's right. You have to go," he said, rubbing his chin. "So when are you coming back?"

She smiled. "Probably the next afternoon. That's Christmas eve," she said looking up at him through her lashes. He was chewing on his lip. "Raleigh, are you pouting?"

"Of course not. Professors don't pout. They brood," he said as he shoved the refrigerator door shut. "But not for long." He went to her, handed her his bottle of beer and began unbuttoning her blouse.

"Can I help you with something?" she asked, holding her peeled tangerine in one hand and his beer in her other.

"No, thanks. I think I know where everything is," he said, pulling her a few inches closer and wrapping her legs around his waist. "We should get started," he said, lifting her off the counter.

"Started with what?" she asked as the beer bottle lightly thumped his back.

"Making up for next Monday night," he said, walking her to the kitchen table.

"No wonder you're a professor," she said, raising her chin to encourage his kisses. "You're so smart about these things."

"Damn right." He kicked a chair out of the way then lowered her on the table. "I miss you already," he said and for that one moment while he spoke she knew he wasn't joking.

Rebecca spotted Raleigh the moment she entered the faculty Christmas party the following Monday night. He'd just backed away from a group of people by the buffet table and was making his way toward her side of the room. The instant he noticed her he stopped dead in his tracks. Looking quickly around, he walked over to her with a twinkle in his eye and a frown on his face.

"Why aren't you at Jade's?"

"Been there and done that, Professor Hanlon," she said, waving at Dean Callahan before meeting Raleigh's gaze. "You look a little pale. You're not having a heart attack, are you?"

"Not yet." His expression grew more confused by the second as he took a look behind him. "Who were you waving at?"

"At Dean Callahan. You know, I haven't crashed this elegant a party in years. Do you think he'll be upset? Well, never mind," she said, reaching out to give Raleigh's arm a squeeze, "we're about to find out."

Raleigh shot her a look of alarm, then rolled his eyes. "Look," he said, leaning close to her ear, "I'll tell him you're my date and that you arrived late."

"You'd lie for me? What a sweetie." She turned and held out her hand to the dean before Raleigh had a chance to answer. "Dean Callahan, it's so nice to see you."

"And you, my dear. I'm delighted you could make it tonight," he said, as several people looked their way. "I trust my directions to this building were clear. It can be difficult getting around the campus if you're not familiar with the area."

"Your directions made it easy, but if they hadn't worked the address is on my invitation," she said, stealing a glance at Raleigh. The crinkles around his eyes were threatening a smile as he shook his head.

Dean Callahan looked at her with a smile of thinly disguised satisfaction. He turned. "Raleigh," he said, as if he'd just come up with an exceptional idea, "why don't you see if Miss Barnett needs anything."

"I was just about to do that, sir." Raleigh gave Rebecca a playfully reprimanding look as the dean started away from them. "Champagne? Crudités? Or perhaps you'd prefer a minute of privacy to wipe that candy-eating grin off your face?"

"No, thanks," she said, giving him a wide-eyed, innocent smile. "I had you going there for second, didn't I?"

"Just for a second."

"Would you like me to check your pulse now?"

"Don't push it," he said, shaking off a smile.

"You actually thought I'd crashed the party, didn't you?"

"I'm not sure what I thought," he said, as he began looking her over with a lover's leisurely eye, "except that since the moment I saw you standing here I knew this party wasn't going to be the same old same old anymore." Rubbing his chin, he looked away. "Tell me, does the word conventional appear anywhere in your personal dictionary?''

She frowned, as a feeling of apprehension mixed with self-doubt rippled through her. She knew Raleigh enjoyed her spontaneity, so why wouldn't he approve of her practical joke? The idea that he might seriously disapprove didn't make sense. This wasn't one of the elaborate pranks of her high school years. She'd planned tonight's surprise for one reason, to share a private laugh with him, her lover.

"Well," she said, fiddling with the clasp on her evening bag as she tried smothering the odd feeling, "I'll take that remark as a compliment. And anyway, I tried telling you that the dean had invited me, too, but you kept insisting I had to go to Jade's party."

"What *was* I thinking of?" he asked as his glance drifted over the low neckline of the curve-clinging, burgundy velvet bodice of her cocktail dress then out toward the other guests. Keeping a chaste distance from her, he gave a long and appreciative sigh.

"Oh, now I get it," she said, raising her evening bag to hide her quiet laughter of relief. "No one here knows we've been having breakfast together for the last week and a half."

He nodded as he looked up at the garland-draped chandeliers. "That's right. If any of them or Dean Callahan suspects we're more than landlord and tenant, we'll be on display the rest of the night. And right now the private pleasure of quietly lusting after you in public excites the hell out of me," he said under his breath.

Turning toward her he gave her a cordial smile. "So, how was Jade's party?" he asked in a conversational tone as several people walked by.

"Fascinating," she said, barely able to contain her smile. "Just fascinating. Jade's brought a gorgeous man back to Follett River with her. She's telling everyone he's her assistant, but Megan and I aren't buying it."

"Why not?"

She wrapped an arm around her waist then ran her thumb over the neckline of her dress. "Oh, I think it's pretty obvious when there's a particular kind of chemistry between two people. Don't you?"

"I'll say," he said, rubbing the back of his neck as he glanced around the room. "By the way, is the skirt on that dress you're wearing made of taffeta?"

"You're very observant tonight, Professor Hanlon," she said, tucking a lock of her hair behind the cluster of sparkling red stones attached to her earlobe. "You're not allergic to taffeta, are you?"

"Who cares? You're worth a rash."

"I love it when you talk dirty to me."

Taking her by the elbow, he guided her behind a thick screen of potted palms and out of view from the rest of the party guests. Backing her against a thick marble column, he gave her a hard, wet kiss that sucked the breath from her. "I was concerned about taffeta making noise if I wanted to run my hand up your leg."

"Silk taffeta doesn't rustle. It whispers," she said licking the taste of him from her lips before she smiled. "Would you like to give it a try?"

Glancing around them, he swore under his breath, then gave her a needy look she'd come to crave. Reaching under her dress, he began inching his hand up the inside of her leg. "You like this walk on the wild side," he said, his gaze heating with forbidden excitement.

"I love it." Boldly curving her hand over his partial arousal, she gave him a gentle squeeze then watched as his lips parted in that way she adored. "Ask me why I love it."

He tried for even breaths as his gaze bore into hers. "Why?"

She reached up with her other hand to slip her fingers into his hair. Urging him closer, she whispered hotly against his ear, "Because you love it."

Raleigh held her close, as his body reacted strongly to her provocative statement and daring touch. Whether he was ready to admit it or not, Rebecca was right. He loved stepping over the edge with her in these tantalizing moments. Loved it so much it scared and thrilled him at the same time.

"Raleigh?"

He pulled back his head from hers.

"Someone's coming." Her sultry smile challenged him not to move.

At the last possible moment Raleigh withdrew his hand from her thigh and stepped back. A second later he nodded at two people walking by them into the ballroom. When he looked back at Rebecca she was smiling triumphantly. He chuckled and shook his head. "I doubt if you could prove I love it as much as you," he said, wondering if she would take his statement as a compliment to her spirited nature or a genuine offer to prove what he said was true. He didn't have to wonder for long.

"You love it so much that if I told you I didn't wear any underwear to this party, you'd have to come up with a way to get me alone and find out."

He swallowed slowly. She wasn't wearing any underwear? He looked her up and down then closed his eyes. "Rebecca . . . ?" When he opened them she was slowly circling around him. "Rebecca," he began again. She gave him a hint of a smile then headed around the potted palms and into the ballroom without him.

When his body was capable of movement, he went after her, catching up with her halfway across the ballroom floor.

"Are you serious?"

She kinked a brow and shrugged.

"So... what? You mean you're not wearing a slip."

"I believe I said underwear, Professor." She gave his arm a friendly pat then looked at her watch. "You'll excuse me. It's getting late, and I haven't spent any time with my host," she said, leaving him in the middle of the ballroom as she headed for Dean Callahan.

Raleigh kept his distance, watching her from across the room and telling himself her joke was too "over the top," even for her. Fifteen minutes later, he was still watching her and wondering if it could be true. He blinked and looked away. Okay, so in that pleasantly outrageous part of his brain, he liked thinking it was true. He liked thinking about it a lot. Pulling on his collar, he cleared his throat then jammed his fists in his pockets. What the hell was wrong with him? He'd been standing around eating goose liver pâté, making small talk and burning out brain cells for fifteen torturous minutes, when he could be proving she was wearing her underwear. Or better yet, proving she wasn't. Excusing himself from the group near the buffet, he strolled over to stand behind her. "You were joking."

She looked over her shoulder at him and, never missing a beat, said, "Not a stitch."

"I'm sorry, Rebecca," Dean Callahan said. "Did you say something?"

"I was just telling Raleigh it felt a little breezy in here."

"These old buildings can be a bit drafty," the white-haired gentleman said. "Don't you agree, Raleigh?"

Raleigh was running a finger around the inside of his collar again. "Pardon...? Yes, it is warm in here." A second later he realized his mistake as all six sets of eyes in the group turned his way. "Of course, I meant cool," he said, settling his gaze on Rebecca. "The, uh, conservatory is just across the hall. They keep it warm in there. Have you seen it yet?"

"No, I haven't."

"Why don't you let me show it to you now?" he asked, silently congratulating himself for coming up with the idea. Just the moonlight, the orchids and Rebecca.

"That sounds lovely. I wish you'd asked me earlier though," she said, frowning as she checked her watch. "My mother's expecting me home soon."

Raleigh stared at her for several seconds before he remembered to close his mouth. "You're leaving?"

"I'm afraid I have to," she said, giving him an enigmatic smile. "I did enjoy our talk a while ago. Perhaps we can get together soon and see what can be done about locating those... missing items."

While he had been wasting time at the buffet table deciding whether or not she was wearing her panties, he'd completely forgotten she'd already told him she was spending the night at her mother's. He could swear a film of perspiration near his hairline was gathering strength and about to run down his forehead in noisy rivulets. Good Lord, he'd seen cartoon characters handle desperation better than this. "I'd like that. How about tomorrow?" he asked, hoping he didn't sound as desperate as he felt.

"Tomorrow? Why don't I call you, Professor, and let you know?"

Tomorrow? Yes! Fine! When? Where? "That would work." Raleigh nodded as Rebecca, a model of graciousness and poise, turned to say goodbye to the people around her and then to thank Dean Callahan for inviting her. When she walked by him a few moments later his ego deflated completely, pricked wide open with her perky I-warned-you grin. She continued across the ballroom floor, disappearing then reappearing like a Christmas dream among the other guests.

Wait! Tell me now. What time are you coming home tomorrow? he wanted to shout. But in a room filled with one hundred faculty members and their guests, that was the last thing, after *fire!* he could see himself shouting.

"She reminds me of Cinderella but with a lot more style," the dean said, as he moved to Raleigh's side. He took in a deep, dramatic breath then let it out as Rebecca slipped on her coat and disappeared out the door. "But instead of a glass slipper, she leaves the scent of her perfume."

Raleigh slowly turned his head toward the white-haired gentleman. He'd worked with him for almost a decade, and only now did he realize what an old romantic the dean was.

Dean Callahan lowered his chin and regarded Raleigh for several seconds. "In my day, young man, I would have skipped the buffet, taken her straight to the solarium and locked the door behind us."

Raleigh looked toward the door again. The old man was right. He and Rebecca should have been locked in the solarium for the last half hour with only the whisper of silk taffeta and her sweet moans for company. What good was a Ph.D. when he couldn't locate a common-sense thought like that? Sliding his hands into his pockets, he didn't bother to stifle his disappointed sigh.

Rebecca waved at Raleigh as he drove into the field beside the old warehouse and parked beside her car.

"I came over as soon as I heard your phone message," he said before he stepped out and shut the door. "Are you okay?"

She nodded.

"You haven't been swinging out over the river on that cable again?" he asked, eyeing her long, corduroy skirt.

She shook her head as he crossed the few feet of snow-covered ground to where she was leaning against her car.

"Okay. Why did you ask me to meet you here this afternoon?" he asked, as he looked up at the huge structure behind her, then gave her a frustrated frown. "This place looks even more dangerous than the last time I saw it. I wish you wouldn't come down here by yourself. Stop and think—"

"I missed you, too," she said, cutting him off. Wrapping her red-gloved hands around his shoulders, she waited for his frustrated expression to soften before she kissed him.

He'd started to deepen the kiss when a flock of noisy pigeons flew off the warehouse roof, startling them both. "Why are we here, Rebecca?"

"You mean, why did I ask you to my side of the river?" she asked, watching him closely. Moving out of his arms, she took a few steps backward to lean against her car. "Last night at the party you started me thinking. One thing led to another," she said, pointing at the warehouse.

"Go on," he said, his carefully composed expression not quite hiding his uneasiness.

"Every time I mention the redevelop project for this property and how I hope to have new office space in it, you suggest I look at downtown Follett River. I know you're only thinking about my welfare, but I thought it was time for you to see this place through my eyes. To look beyond its spotted history and imagine what it can become."

Raising his brows, he shrugged. "As long as you got me over here . . ."

Pointedly ignoring his reluctant attitude, she took his hand and led him past abandoned machinery and rusty oil drums toward the front of the building. "The Macleod estate is over there," she said, letting go of him to point across the river, "and since they'll never sell off any of it, that beautiful woodland view is permanent." Turning to face him again, her long coat flapped open, causing her below-the-knee-length skirt to puff and snap in the bracing breeze. "How does it sound so far?"

Raleigh's skeptical stare began softening as he looked around him. "Okay."

"Okay? Well, try not to break into song until you've seen the inside."

He looked at the No Trespassing sign, then shifted his gaze toward her. "Rebecca . . ."

"And, just for a minute, pretend you didn't see that," she said, motioning him toward the warehouse door.

Expecting a dark and gloomy interior, Raleigh followed her inside. Instead he found the space filled with thick, angled shafts of sunlight that were streaming in from the upper windows. A sturdy web of exposed girders and vertical supports provided a crisscross of shadows on the dry cement floor. He nodded once. "Well, it's . . . big."

She caught his gaze, then gave him a mischievous grin. "And you know how I love big things."

"I seem to recall your penchant for that."

She allowed herself one laugh then gestured with her arms. Her teasing tone disappeared, replaced with a voice that demanded serious listening. "Picture the front of the building in mostly glass and the space we're in right now a giant atrium. Two floors of commercial businesses will be facing the atrium so they'll all have a river view."

He listened as she talked on about building materials, several possible completion dates and where she wanted her office. As always, her enthusiasm was contagious. When he turned to look around, he realized his attitude about the once-forbidding place was already changing. Rebecca was leading him to imagine all sorts of impressive possibilities. She'd accomplished the astonishing feat with humor, originality and her own distinctive brand of charm.

Suddenly he wasn't listening to her sales pitch anymore. He was too busy coming to the all-powerful truth about the woman delivering it. With his back toward her, he allowed his private smile to turn to quiet laughter.

For weeks he'd been telling himself she was a pleasing surprise, a breath of fresh air, a rare and renewing force in his life. And the only person who had ever tapped into the passionate part of him. But that wasn't the half of it. The bigger picture he was coming to see wasn't about office space and river views. He rubbed at his mouth then shoved his hand through his hair as the realization began to take a firm hold. He was in love with her.

"You're right," he said, staring blankly toward the back of the building. "Once, I viewed this place as little more than an accident waiting to happen. But in your own special way, you've made me take a second look."

"I'm so glad to hear you say that. Convincing you to take that second look was one of the reasons I asked you here."

He felt his brow wrinkling. "One of the reasons?" He began to turn as she walked into his field of vision. Confidence radiated from her smile like heat from a heat lamp. A pair of bikini panties dangled from the fingertips of her red kid gloves.

"I know the idea isn't a ... conventional one, but you said last night that *conventional* wasn't to be found in my personal dictionary."

He looked around the cavernous space, then at the panties and finally at her. "Are you talking about the redevelopment project or are you suggesting ... ?"

She smiled, then jiggled her hand that held the panties. There was no mistaking what she had in mind. He looked toward the door as the first ripple of excitement shot through him. "Here?" he asked, not quite able to stop his smile. "Rebecca, I don't know about this."

Wrapping her fingers around his tie, she began backing toward a hip-high, wooden platform with him in tow. "No guts, no glory." Bumping the edge, she said, "Right here feels fine."

"Anyone could walk in," he said, looking around them as he took the panties from her hand and stuffed them in his pocket.

"Kind of exciting, isn't it?" she said, pulling a condom packet from her pocket, then running it along his belt buckle.

"Kind of," he agreed as he picked her up, set her on the platform and kissed her. "Damn you, Rebecca, you can start me up with one smile."

"I love it when you finally decide to do something," she said, setting the condom packet beside her as she shrugged out of her coat. "You get that nothing-can-stop-me look in your eyes."

"So do you," he said, as he began to unbutton her blouse.

"These hard decisions are the best." Pulling off her gloves, she tossed them behind her before reaching to embrace him.

"The best," he agreed as he began pressing hungry kisses down the side of her neck. When she opened her blouse and urged his mouth lower, Raleigh heard himself groaning with pleasure. *She wasn't wearing any underwear.* In the chilly air her breasts felt like warm silk to his cool lips, but soon that luxurious sensation wasn't enough. He wanted the temperature raised.

So did she.

Sinking her fingers into his hair, she nibbled his ear. "I need you so much. Hurry, Raleigh."

Making love to Rebecca had always proved adventurous, but never more so than in this improbable place. Reaching beneath her skirt, he parted her legs then rubbed his thumbs along the insides of her thighs. The thought of sinking himself inside her intimate embrace had his desire for her skyrocketing. "Rebecca, are you sure about this?"

"Can't you tell?" she whispered, arching toward him as he moved his hands higher. When his fingers brushed her hot, moist center, she let out a breathy moan that made a pearly cloud in the air between them.

"I want you closer," she said, running her hand over the distinct ridge behind his zipper.

If her bold stroke hadn't sealed their fate, her next move did. Leaning back, she planted her hands behind her in a move of wanton surrender. His hands stopped moving as he looked at her, framed by her red wool coat and white silk blouse. Her beautiful face, her tight, rosy nipples and the soft curves of her body, all lay waiting for him in a shaft of platinum-tinged sunlight. Reaching out, he drew his fingers over one nipple, then watched it quiver when he released it. Every second with her was a gift. She'd brought him back to life, and now he couldn't imagine it without her. Leaning down, he thanked her with a kiss that left them both gasping.

"Please, Raleigh," she said with unbridled desire ringing through her words, "make it happen."

"You know I can't say no to you." Withdrawing his hands from her thighs, he reached for the condom packet and began tearing it open. "Pull up your skirt," he said, then paused to watch her move the dark material above her knees. "Take it higher," he said, unzipping his pants then readying himself with the condom. "A little more. Yes," he said, moving between her legs. He'd never wanted anyone like he wanted her. But more than wanting her, he'd begun to crave her. Ache for her.

Alone in the warehouse, with the sound of the rushing river mixing with her sweet moans, he wrapped himself fully in the steamy warmth of her satin clasp. When he whispered her name, she contracted against him. His shudder of surprise prompted her to repeat the act until he began to move within her. "Is this what you wanted?"

"Yes," she cried, dropping her head back.

With stroke after surging stroke, he brought her to the edge, then joined her in a stunning climax while their cries echoed around them.

Nine

"Can I take it off?" Rebecca asked, lifting her chin and leaning forward in the chair. The blindfold he'd tied around her eyes was doing its job well. She couldn't see a thing.

"Not yet," Raleigh said from somewhere near her feet.

"I promised my mother I'd be over at her place by seven-thirty," she said, scratching the bridge of her nose beneath the bandana. "They said they wouldn't be able to keep my nephews away from their presents for much longer than that. Can I take this off now?"

"Just a little longer."

From his voice and the occasional shuffling sounds, Rebecca could tell he was doing something close to the floor. She tapped her fingers on her knees as she fought the urge to peek. "I'd forgotten how worked up little boys can get over this holiday. They were threatening to

take their flashlights and camp out on the roof last night
to make sure Santa knew which chimney was theirs.
Raleigh, are you almost done down there?''

"Now who's getting worked up? You've got the worst
case of Christmas-morning curiosity I've ever seen.''

"Well, what do you expect, dragging me blindfolded
into the library at quarter to six in the morning? You've
got me as curious as a five-year-old.''

"Five-year-old? I thought you said six.''

"Six what?'' she asked, touching the red bandana at
her temples. Before he answered, she heard a soft electric buzz and then a clackety-clacking. She pulled in a
sharp breath when she pictured the only thing that could
make such a sound. Her heart thumped wildly as she
clutched her fists to her chest. "Oh, you didn't,'' she
could barely whisper.

"You can take off the blindfold.''

Before he'd finished giving her permission, she pulled
the cloth from her eyes and was scrambling to her knees.

He laughed as she gave an impressive scream then
pointed at the shiny, eight-car train set. As the lead car
emitted its miniature puff of steam, the train took a
curve into a tunnel under the far side of the Christmas
tree. A few seconds later it emerged from the other end,
then headed through a tiny town and toward her. "Is it
really all mine?'' she asked, first pressing her hands to
her cheeks, then locking her fingers together beneath her
chin.

"It's really all yours.''

"Oh, Raleigh, thank you!''

"Watch this,'' Raleigh said, as the red lights flashed,
the train whistled and the crossing gate lowered. When
the train came to the crossing, Raleigh eased it to a stop.
"Your cap, Madame Engineer,'' he said, tossing her one

with traditional navy-and-white stripes. "Think you're ready to take the controls?"

"Just watch me, sonny, and one day Santa might bring you your own set," she said, settling the cap on her head at a jaunty if not traditional angle. Crawling over to Raleigh on her hands and knees, she twisted around to sit between his legs.

"Hey, I like that move," he said, as he pulled her back into his arms for a kiss. "I like this move, too."

She looked up at him for a long moment before swallowing hard and turning her face toward the train set. "I think you've finally done it, Hanlon."

"What's that?" he asked, kissing the side of her neck.

"Overwhelmed me," she said, as tears began moistening her eyes.

"I hope so," he said with a teasing roll of his eyes. "It's six in the morning and I've been up for the last hour setting this up. Hey. You're not going to cry, are you?"

"I can if I want," she said dabbing her eyes with the pink chenille tie to her robe. "I might have my own train set now, but I'm still a girl."

He wrapped his arms around her then sniffed at her neck. "You're right. You're still a girl. But I have to tell you, I almost didn't give this to you."

She laughed and brushed away a tear. "Why? Haven't I been naughty enough?"

"Lord knows, you've been that, but I had so much fun picking it out I thought about keeping it and letting you run it every now and then. Of course, I was smart enough to soon realize you'd never settle for sharing it," he said with a teasing wink, as she reached for the controls and started the train moving again. After several hair-raising runs around the oval track, she pulled to a neat stop by a farmyard.

"If you're that smart, would you mind explaining why there are four dalmatians grazing in my meadow?"

"Because the toy store was out of cows. You don't miss much, do you?"

Never taking her gaze from the train, she smiled as she lifted a dalmatian into the cattle car then settled her hands back on the control box. Running the engine at top speed once again, she made several whistle-screaming trips around the track, then she brought the cars to a perfect stop in front of the station. Throwing up her hands, she announced, "And nobody got hurt!"

Raleigh playfully collapsed against her shoulder from feigned exhaustion. "Are you sure?"

"Hmm. There's not a nurse's kit in sight, but I'd be happy to examine you, anyway... after you open your gifts. What did you do with the packages I put next to the tree the other day?"

"Under this table," he said, pointing behind them.

She reached for the top one. "Now that you've shared this Freudian moment with me, I'm sure this won't be half as exciting," she said, pressing the package into his hand. "But go ahead and open it anyway."

"I'll pretend to be pleased," he said, peeling away the foil paper and lifting out the gift. He pulled in a fast breath then lifted his eyes to hers. "*The Conquest of Peru* by Prescott." Opening the book, he checked the printing date. "Where did you find one this old?"

"In a book shop in Greenwich Village. They told me it was printed around the turn of the century." She smiled as she watched him run his fingers along the spine of the leather-bound copy, and then she leaned in to give him a kiss.

"You remembered that conversation we had the night of my party," he said with a slightly stunned tone to his voice.

"Raleigh," she said, tracing his lips with her thumb, "I remember every word you've ever told me." The moment resonated between them, rich with unspoken emotion.

Setting the book aside, he took off her railroad cap and slipped his fingers into her hair. The warm heels of his hands cushioned her jaw while his intimate stare caressed the rest of her face. "How you continue to amaze," he said, his voice raspy with emotion.

She covered his hand with hers. "And you're the best Christmas surprise I've ever had."

"Come here," he said, pulling her into his arms.

Melting into his masculine caress, she rested her cheek in the now familiar spot beneath his shoulder. Why had she ever allowed herself to doubt his opinion of her? He was the most affectionate, loving and thoughtful man she'd ever known. "Merry Christmas, Mr. Hanlon," she said, wishing the precious moment could last forever. The soft, silent laughter rumbling through him, made her want to snuggle closer.

"Merry Christmas, Miss Barnett."

The moment ended on twin groans when the phone rang. Releasing her, Raleigh checked his watch, stood up and walked the few steps to his desk. "Weird time to call," he mumbled, looking back at her as he reached for the phone. He made a comically fearful face. "Maybe you haven't been as naughty as you could. Maybe Santa wants the train back."

Rebecca narrowed her eyes and dropped her chin in a warning look that meant "Don't even think about it." He winked, then answered the phone with a "Merry

Christmas.'' A few seconds later she watched his amused expression disappear.

Shoving his fingers through his hair, he turned away from Rebecca. ''What hospital?... Try to calm down, Celia...I'm sure she's going to be fine. Yes, of course you were right to call me. I'm coming right over.''

Rebecca was on her feet and closing the space between them, before he could turn back to her. ''What is it?''

''Penny,'' he said, blinking as he shoved his fingers through his hair again, then held on to it. ''She's been in some kind of an accident. Her mother doesn't have the complete story yet.''

''Raleigh, I'm so sorry,'' she whispered, as he slid his arm around her shoulders. His painful gaze tore at her insides, but he somehow managed a scant half smile in acknowledgment of her concern.

''How badly is she hurt?'' When his only response was to stare into space, her own fears began multiplying. She turned his face toward her. ''Raleigh, what did the doctor say?''

Raleigh focused on her. ''He's in with her now. I told Celia I'd be right over. Rebecca...''

''I'll go with you.''

He looked hard at her as he began to bring his scattered emotions under control. ''It's okay. Everything will be okay,'' he said, even as his gaze lost its focus again. ''You've, uh, got to get over to your mother's—''

''Raleigh, I'm going with you.'' When he suddenly focused on her, she realized her voice had been tinged with alarm. ''Of course, I'm sure Penny's going to be fine,'' she said in the most reassuring tone she could muster. ''I'll drive us.''

"No," he said, his voice suddenly firm. "There's probably no reason to panic. I'm dressed. I'll go now, and you can meet me there when you're ready. And this way, once we know Penny's okay, you'll be able to go on to your family for Christmas morning with them." He dropped a kiss on her forehead, then took her in his arms for an unbearably brief hug. "This will all work out."

When Rebecca found him in the emergency waiting room, he stopped his pacing and held out his arms to her. His grateful look nearly made her cry.

"How is she?"

"I don't know. They won't let me in," he said, glaring at the nurses' station down the hall. "Dammit, I'm her uncle."

He began rubbing her shoulders, a soothing move, she knew, as much for him as for herself. "Did you find out what happened?"

He shrugged impatiently. "I don't know all of it, but it seems she was climbing something and she fell. The police called her mother a few hours ago. Celia didn't realize she'd left the house until then." Raleigh sank down on the couch and leaned forward, his elbows on his knees. "Rebecca, she's so much like Buddy, she scares me."

Rebecca shrugged out of her coat and sat down beside him. "You never really told me about him," she said, hoping to get his mind off Penny and the nerve-wracking wait to find out how she was. "What was he like?"

Raleigh thought for a moment, then gave a short laugh and shook his head. "Funny. You remind me of him, too. At least, when you were younger," he said, smiling at his recollections. He played with the back of her hair. "He was always smiling. Buddy loved a good practical joke, whether he was playing it on someone or it was played on him. He loved his mischief." Raleigh pressed a fist to his chin and looked down. "He loved it too much. He didn't know when enough was enough. There was a wild streak in him." He stopped to take in a breath, then let it out in a weary sigh. "I see that same streak in Penny. That's why I've watched her like I have. If anything happens— What am I saying?" he asked, suddenly standing. "It *has* happened."

"You can't keep blaming yourself for this. It wasn't your fault that she fell, just like it wasn't your fault that Buddy died."

He looked at her for a long, troubled moment, as if he wanted to tell her something but couldn't. A dozen strange thoughts ran through her mind. "What is it? What haven't you told me?"

"Rebecca, I—" he began, then swung around as a door at the opposite side of the room opened.

"Celia. How is she?"

The woman, an older, worried version of Penny, waved Raleigh into the room. Her pained expression had Raleigh biting off a curse as he let go of Rebecca and headed for the opened door.

The longest fifteen minutes of Rebecca's life dragged by. She soon gave up grilling the nurses about Penny's condition when they began avoiding her. Instead she paced the waiting room, wondering about Raleigh and what he hadn't told her. As the minutes ticked by, the possibilities racing through her mind grew crazier. Was Penny Raleigh's daughter? Had Raleigh caused Buddy's death? Or was Buddy alive somewhere and no one but Raleigh knew about it? She shook her head at the last thought. This wasn't a television soap opera. Speculating was getting her nowhere. She would simply have to wait for Raleigh. But, dammit, he could have told her long before this. No, that wasn't fair. Besides, she knew he *was* ready to tell her, and when she saw him, she had no doubt he would.

She looked up as the door swung open. Raleigh walked out of the room, a grim set to his lips, a hard look in his eyes.

"Is she all right?" Rebecca asked.

"She broke her arm and they're deciding now whether or not to operate."

"But she'll be fine. Right?"

A muscle moved in his jaw.

"What is it?" she asked, as a new kind of alarm went through her. "What aren't you telling me?"

"She could have broken her neck," he said, still staring hard at her. "She and a couple of friends decided to climb the Daleville water tower to spray-paint a message to her classmates. On the way down she slipped and fell. She lay on the hard ground for thirty minutes."

"Oh, Raleigh, I'm so sorry," she said, reaching out for him.

"There's more," he said, holding up his hand to keep her away. "She said she'd gotten the idea from you. That you told her you'd done the same thing when you were her age."

"Oh, no," she said, pressing her hands to her face. "I didn't think—"

He turned on her then, his voice a fierce whisper ripping at her heart. "That's just it. You didn't think, Rebecca. I left you two alone for five minutes and you managed to tell her that story. You didn't stop to think about how she would react. She could have been killed," he said, slamming his hand against the wall. "Just like Buddy."

"I'm so sorry," she said, taking her shaking hands from her face. Leaning back against the wall, she wrapped her arms around her middle and waited for the wave of nausea to pass.

"Didn't it occur to you that when someone that young looks up to you, you have an obligation, a duty to behave in a responsible way?" He shook his head, turning away in what she could only imagine was disgust. "Things never change."

His last words went through her heart like a well-aimed dagger. What he meant and wasn't saying was that *she* had never changed. That in his eyes, she was still the reckless teenager who had caused him grief then as now. That maybe the spiked hair and motorcycle jacket were gone, but she was still the same irresponsible Reb Barnett. Only this time someone he loved had almost died because of her.

There was no use talking to Raleigh, and even if there were, she was still reeling from his accusations. She looked around the room, surprised to see the walls and furniture unchanged. The nurse at the station across the hall was marking her chart. The fish in the small aquarium continued moving slowly through their watery world. A disembodied voice came over the loudspeaker to direct a doctor to the orthopedic floor. No one and nothing appeared to know or care that the world, as she had come to know it, was collapsing around her. "I'll go." She made it to the door, then turned back. "Will you tell Penny's mother..."

The look of pain in his red-rimmed eyes was too much. She shook her head. "Never mind," she said, pushing open the door and walking into a biting wind.

* * *

The rest of Christmas was a blur filled with other people's laughter. Even the usually hilarious antics of her young nephews failed to pull her away from her thoughts about Raleigh and his niece. She managed to call the hospital several times, and when she was finally assured that Penny wouldn't need surgery, her relief soon turned to emotional and physical exhaustion. She made it through dinner, then told her family she wasn't feeling well and headed back to the little apartment over Raleigh's garage.

Like a dazed accident victim herself, she sat in her kitchen, hoping for a knock on her door. A knock that she knew in her heart wouldn't come.

Was he right? Had she been irresponsible by telling Penny about her own prank? And if so, had she been wrong about other things as well?

She pulled on her coat and sat out on the landing, looking over at Raleigh's house. Their entire relationship had had a fantasylike quality about it. Why hadn't Raleigh talked more about his brother? About himself? What was the big secret?

She blew on her hands to keep them warm. No matter how beautiful, how intense, how wonderful the time they'd shared together seemed to be, Raleigh had been careful to keep a closed mouth about his life. In fact, Megan had told her more about Raleigh's brother than he had. Raleigh was as buttoned down as his shirts about his own life. And everything in it.

Everything and everyone. Like her. Standing slowly, she turned and went inside as the truth began to rise to her consciousness. While he'd kept her to himself, he had also been keeping her away from the rest of his life. Dropping her coat on a kitchen chair, she slapped away a tear and headed for the sun room sofa. That was it, that was the answer to all of it. Things were fine when they were alone and passion ruled their lives, but that was as far as he'd ever wanted it to go. He'd never shown any interest in going public with their relationship.

It would be easy to think he would be this way with any woman, easy to understand how difficult it was for him to let anyone fully into his life after such a long time. But she wasn't stupid. Not only had his opinion of her never changed, he'd kept their relationship apart from the rest of his life because she was an embarrassment to him. His shameful secret. The lover who had come from the wrong side of the river. His former student whom he had to keep separate from the other, more important, parts of his life. She waited for the anger to rise up so she could blot out the humiliating thoughts, but anger never came. Only a scalding hurt that took her breath. She'd changed. She'd grown up and was a responsible, caring person. It was Raleigh Hanlon who hadn't changed, because in his eyes she was still trouble.

Penny was sitting up in bed, the remote control to the television poised in midair when Rebecca walked in.

"Hi!" Penny said.

"Hi, yourself, young lady," she said as she crossed the room and set a stack of magazines on the hospital bedside table beside a calculus textbook. "These magazines are for when you're not studying."

"Thanks," Penny said, clicking off the television.

"That's an awesome cast you have there," she said, pointing to it. "How are you feeling?"

"I'll live, but the worst is yet to come. Uncle Raleigh says when I'm allowed to go home he's coming over to give me the lecture of my life."

Rebecca nodded. "Well, at least he's talking to you."

"He's blaming you for this, isn't he? That is so stupid," she said. "Don't feel too bad though. My mom says he was no angel when he was young, either."

Rebecca raised her brows at Penny's last comment, but decided not to question her about it. Raleigh had once told her he'd raised a little hell himself, but she'd never quite believed him. The important thing now was that Penny was feeling well enough to make a convoluted attempt at comforting her visitor.

"We've all acted pretty stupid, Penny. I probably shouldn't have mentioned my little escapade, and you shouldn't have acted on it."

Penny rolled her eyes. "I don't get it. I was the one who screwed up, but all you adults want to do is share the blame. My mom thinks because she didn't come into my bedroom every hour to check on me, you know, like she did when I was a baby, that this was her fault. *You* feel bad just because you told me a good story. And Uncle Raleigh's walking around with a four-star guilt crown on his head because he says he wasn't there for me like he wasn't there for my father." She shook her head. "You adults are so messed up."

Rebecca's slight smile froze when a curious tightening started in the pit of her stomach. She casually tucked a lock of hair behind one ear and leaned forward in her chair. "Penny, what do you think your uncle meant when he said he wasn't there for your father?"

"I don't know. He says things like that all the time," she said with a shrug that collapsed into a wince. Cautiously touching the multicolored bruise on her forehead, Penny let out a sharp yelp.

"Are you okay?" Rebecca asked, coming off the chair and over to the bed in one gliding move. "Do you want me to get your nurse?"

"No," Penny said, gesturing impatiently with her hand. "What I want to know is why grown-ups spend so much time trying to fix what they did and didn't do when they were young." Penny looked up at her. "And why they have to involve us in that stuff."

Rebecca sat down slowly in her chair. "Out of love," she said softly, as the pieces suddenly began falling into place. Could what she was thinking be true?

"But when something's over, it's over. Isn't it? I mean you can't go back and fix what's in the past."

"This isn't over," she said, looking up at Penny. "Look, I meant to stay longer and talk with you," she said, standing up and moving quickly for the door. "I'll come back, but I have something to do that can't wait."

Ten

When Raleigh didn't answer his doorbell, Rebecca didn't hesitate to use the house key he'd given her. Walking down the hall, she stood at the bottom of the staircase and called out his name. The only sound was the hum from the heating system. She'd wait, she told herself as she pulled off her coat and turned toward the library. If it meant missing her high school reunion later that night, she was determined to find out if what she'd started to suspect was true.

Dropping her coat on the back of the library sofa, she looked around the room. The unlighted Christmas tree made a sad and lonely display in the purple shadows of the late afternoon. Walking a few steps closer to the tree, she stopped to smooth her hands along the worn spot on the back of the leather chair where Raleigh had rested his head. How many times, she wondered, had she walked into this room in the last month to find him reading portions of his manuscript or grading student papers? And how many times had she tossed aside what was in his hands, then sat on his lap and snuggled with him?

"Too many?" she whispered to herself, as she glanced away at the glowing embers in the fireplace. Stiffening her resolve to stay and wait for answers, she walked around the room. It wouldn't be too long before Raleigh would be showing up. He'd left a fire burning, and because of his cautious nature, he'd have to come back soon and check on it.

Walking by his neatly filled bookshelves, she smiled at the thought that this library had once intimidated her to the point of staying out of it...until Raleigh had asked her in. Shaking her head, she went to the fireplace, poked at the embers, then carefully added a few pieces of wood.

When she turned to warm her backside by the fire, she spotted an open photo album on the sofa. A photo of Raleigh and a young teenager caught her eye. A moment later she was sitting on the sofa, dragging the heavy album onto her lap. "He must have been looking at these," she mumbled to herself as she started thumbing through. The pages were filled with photos and articles about Raleigh's brother, Buddy. She stopped turning the pages when she found a newspaper clipping detailing an account of how Buddy died.

Her hands were shaking by the time she closed the album and set it aside. When she heard Raleigh walking into the kitchen a few minutes later, she stood up and waited for him. She knew his habits like she knew her own. He would be coming into the library any moment now, a scotch and water in one hand and his reading glasses in the other. And then she would ask the questions that needed answering. There was no other way, nor should there be, she thought.

"You look surprised to see me," she said, as he walked into the library. "Did you think I'd simply go away?"

His open mouth quickly closed to make a firm, grim line. "This isn't a good idea, Rebecca," he said, turning as if to leave.

"Hold on. I won't let you avoid this by backing yourself into that tweed and steel cocoon."

Setting his drink on the table and his reading glasses in his shirt pocket, he eyed her uneasily. "Tweed and steel cocoon? I don't know what you're talking about."

"Sure you do. The one tagged 'aloof and brooding professor, do not touch' that you spun around yourself almost two decades ago."

He waited a long moment to speak. "What do you want to talk about, Rebecca?" he said too quietly.

"About the night your brother died." She could have kneed him in the groin and he wouldn't have looked more surprised. Reaching down, she picked up the album and held it high for him to see.

"What—where did you . . . Rebecca." He dragged a heavy hand over his face.

"You think you killed him, don't you?"

"Don't do this," he said, reaching over the couch to take the album from her.

She pulled it out of his reach so that his hand came down with a smacking sound on the back of the leather sofa.

"You're not going to make this easy, are you?" he asked, shaking his head.

"I've never done anything the easy way, so don't expect me to start now. Tell me what happened that night."

"My brother died," he said, his words coming rapidly on the end of her question.

"And?"

"And what? You want details?" he asked, his voice rising with a snap as he stood up. "All right, one night after a football game, he and his friends got their hands on a couple of six-packs. After they finished them, Buddy decided it might be a hoot to walk the bridge rail over near Daleville." Raleigh looked away, but kept on talking. "I got there in time to see him fall."

"The newspaper story said he clung to an underpinning and was still holding on when you got down there."

"Rebecca, what is this leading to?"

Ignoring his question, she continued, "It says here you risked your life trying to reach him to pull him out. That the others had to hold you back to keep you from going in after him once he let go."

"Why are you doing this?" he asked, moving around the sofa toward her. "He's been dead for nineteen years."

Slamming the album shut, she set it firmly on the bookshelf. "So have you."

"He was my brother," he said, his voice sounding more like a growl. "I have a right..."

"A right to what?" she shot back as she slapped her hand on the album cover. "To carry this overblown sense of guilt around as if it were Buddy's tombstone? Raleigh, you didn't encourage him to climb onto that bridge rail. You didn't pour the beer down his throat that put him up there in the first place. Why can't you stop trying to make up for something that wasn't your fault? Why can't you let this go?"

"Because I bought the beer." The words hung in the air like the echoing ring from a lead-cast bell. Raleigh rubbed his mouth, then turned and walked away from her. There, he'd told her what he'd kept hidden for almost two decades. What no one had ever suspected. What no one else had ever known but Buddy. And he didn't feel one damned bit better. He gave a short, bitter laugh. Where was that cathartic rush he'd fantasized about over the years? Where was the relief of "sharing the pain"?

From the corner of his eye he could see her fiddling with the bottom edge on her bright pink sweater as she slowly paced in front of the fire. Her beauty and her intensity could threaten his resolve, if he allowed it. He steeled himself against the thought.

"Is that it? Are you satisfied?"

Her head came up on his sharp tone. "Did he ask you to buy the beer for him?"

He might as well satisfy her morbid curiosity now, because, knowing Rebecca, she wouldn't stop until she had her answers. "No," he said with a weary sigh. "I was legal age and had bought beer for a party later on that night. A few days after the accident I put two and two together and realized he'd lifted those six-packs from my car trunk."

"So Buddy knew you had beer in the trunk and he *chose* to take it. He *chose* to drink it. And he *chose* to walk that rail," she said in a deliberately methodical manner.

"It wasn't that simple."

"I think it was."

"You weren't there. You don't know what you're talking about. You didn't know him."

"No, I'll never know him like you did, but I've spent the last hour going through those albums. I read the clippings. And those childhood photos...in almost every

one Buddy was looking up at you as if you were his
hero... even when you were no angel yourself.''

He felt a muscle tightening in his jaw. "I never told
you that I was perfect.''

"You never told me anything. But that fact is a part
of it, too, isn't it? You think if you hadn't been such a
hell-raiser yourself, Buddy wouldn't have tried so hard
to copy you and end up failing. That's what the stern,
demanding, Show-No-Mercy Hanlon act comes from.
Trying to make amends for—''

"Are you through?''

"Just about. Look, I'm not saying he was bad, or that
you were, either. If I'd been around back then, we all
probably would have gotten on well together.''

"What the hell have you been doing in here? Figur-
ing out dates on a calculator?''

She moved closer, her voice gentling with what he
knew was genuine compassion. "I know you loved him,
and I can't imagine how terrible it must have been that
night, but isn't it time you buried the boy?''

He narrowed his eyes as her words caught him off
guard, piercing through all nineteen carefully lived years
of penance as if it were rice paper. No. He shook his
head, refusing to be pulled into her Pollyanna scenario.
"Bury him?'' he asked sharply. "And then what do you
want me to do, Rebecca? Tell you it's okay for *you* not
to feel guilty about what happened to Penny? Is that
what this is all about?''

"For your information, I care about Penny, but the
bottom line is, I'm not responsible for what she did.
Penny made her own choice that night just like Buddy
made his. What you're refusing to accept is that there
has to be a point when you stop holding their hands.

They were both over eighteen, eligible to vote and licensed to drive when they made their choices."

She moved a few steps toward him. "Choices, Raleigh. Good or bad ones, we all make choices. Don't you get it?" she asked softly. "It was *his* choice that led to his death. Not yours."

She began reaching out to him but changed her mind and clasped her hands to her breastbone instead. "Raleigh, listen to me, you have a choice now," she whispered with enough passion to make his searching gaze stop and lock with hers. "Let go of this guilt that was never yours to start with."

On some level he knew her words sounded sane, right and sensible, but those truths didn't stop Buddy's face from coming back to him. Buddy and all that black, swirling water. Buddy and the terrified look in his eyes as that water took him under. And this time was worse. This time he could smell the river, feel the cold sweat on his back, taste the panic.

Closing his eyes, he struggled to change the ending, to picture Buddy taking his hand, then holding on until he could pull him to safety. God, if he could change the past.... Just another inch. *I'll get you out. Just take my hand, Buddy. Buddy, take my hand!* But Buddy fell away again.

He rubbed his brow, then shook his head trying to rid himself of the terrible image. Going through it this last time was the worst, and he found himself wanting to lash out like never before.

When he opened his eyes, Rebecca was there, and that reality brought more pain and regret. He could never be the man she wanted, the man she needed, the man she deserved. Why had he ever allowed himself to entangle her in an affair that would only bring her heartbreak?

"You're assuming that because we stumbled into this...time together that you now understand my life. But you can't understand, because we're coming from two different places. You can't possibly—"

She held up her hand for him to stop. "That's enough," she said, lifting her chin, "you don't have to say any more." Backing away from him, she reached for her coat. "Don't worry, I won't be around to embarrass you much longer," she said crisply. "Congratulations, you get your world back all to yourself, Raleigh," she said, turning away from him as she put on her coat and made a business of buttoning it with her back still to him. Reaching into her pocket she brought out his house key and tossed it on the sofa table. "I'll drop my apartment key in your mail box tomorrow morning before I go." She started to leave but stopped when she got to the hall. "Oh, and contrary to what you might have thought, I've never been one for casual flings. I didn't stumble into this relationship with you. Wrong or right, I chose to be with you."

Raleigh stood looking at the empty doorway for a long time after she left. Rebecca was right about one thing: she never did things the easy way. She'd emptied both barrels at him, then pitched a few well-aimed rocks for good measure. As final as her parting words sounded, an emotional numbness prevented him from accepting them. Too much was going down right now for him to think anything was real.

He was still shaking when he walked over to where she'd placed the photo album, brought it back to his chair and slipped on his reading glasses. Opening it, he squinted as he held the album closer. Why was it so hard to make out the once clear images? He switched on a lamp and rubbed at his eyes beneath his glasses, but the photographs were no clearer. Great. A slight touch of hysterical blindness was all he needed.

He looked over his glasses at the Christmas tree, and the apple ornament Rebecca had given him instantly caught his eye. The shiny red sequins and green glass leaves came into sharp focus, sparkling beautifully in the flickering light from the fireplace. He looked back at the page of photos in his lap. Why hadn't he noticed it before? In the natural order of things, the color images were fading.

A fuzzy sensation welled up in his chest and then his throat. He swallowed but the sensation continued. What had Rebecca said?

"Isn't it time you buried the boy?"

Raleigh lifted his gaze from the page, took off his glasses and stared at the empty doorway, this time until his eyes began to sting. After almost two decades, could the end of it be this simple? Was Rebecca right, as she had been about so many things? Could he choose to change the way he'd been living his life? Was it possible to walk away from that bridge? He looked down at the album, but instead of turning another page, he gently closed it and ran his palm over the cover. Rebecca, who had brought love with all its joys and challenges into his life, was right.

"It's time, Buddy," he whispered.

Fifteen minutes later Raleigh was standing at her door, waiting for her to answer his knock. Waiting for a second chance. A chance he wasn't going to blow.

His heartbeat quickened when he saw her through the curtains as she came through the kitchen. Halfway across the floor, she recognized him and stopped. So did

Raleigh's heart. They both started moving again a second later.

"I'm busy," she was saying as she opened the door in her pink chenille robe and towel-turbaned head.

Before he could respond, she went on, her puffy eyes focused on some spot over his shoulder. "In case you've forgotten, and I'm sure you have, my high school reunion's tonight." Hugging the edge of the door, she managed to keep a stranglehold on her robe's collar as she looked down at her bare toes. "That was the reason I came back to Follett River."

"I know that." Actually he *had* known that, but hadn't thought about the event in days. He pointed to her tear-reddened eyes. "Rebecca, I'm sorry—"

"I know, I know," she said, shaking her head. "But you won't be able to be my date. Well, we both knew even before our talk in the library that you would have come up with a last-minute excuse not to go with me."

He opened his mouth to speak, but she cut him off.

"You're off the hook. That's right. You don't have to suffer the embarrassment of being caught with Reb Barnett. Sure, a few people know we've been seeing each other, but don't worry. There's no proof that the girl from the wrong side of the river ever got close to you. No one's ever claimed that, anyway," she said, shutting the door, then opening it again. "And if someone had, who would believe it?" she asked before slamming the door again.

Disregarding the wind whipping at his jacket, he looked out from the landing at the unbroken field of snow covering the yards in his neighborhood.

He couldn't have been more surprised if she'd opened the door, reeled back and thrown an ice-covered snowball at him. The kind of pain he'd seen in her face and

heard in her voice told him she'd believed for a long time
that he was embarrassed to be seen with her. Nothing
could be further from the truth. He'd kept her to himself because he'd selfishly wanted the time to enjoy her
privately. And what a time they'd had. He knew he
wasn't wrong about that. Not with the memories of her
smiles and laughter, her sense of humor, her giving acts
of love.

Dammit, how was he going to convince her that she
had made a terrible mistake thinking he'd been ashamed
of her? Looking back at the door, he considered kicking it open, walking in and announcing just that. Then
he thought better of the idea. She'd always been a head-
strong student; arguing with her had never worked. Besides, while he'd been tearing down emotional walls,
Rebecca had been building one of her own. The one
meant to keep a distance between the two of them. He
exhaled sharply. What had he expected? She'd learned
by example. His example. There was only one thing to
do now. Change the lesson plan to fit the student.
Checking his watch, he glanced again at her door then
headed down the steps.

Rebecca looked around the Follett River High School
gymnasium, filled with former classmates, curtains of
crepe paper streamers and enough memories of Show-
No-Mercy Hanlon to bring on a migraine.

Trying not to think about Raleigh was a nearly impossible feat. His name had popped up half a dozen
times since she'd arrived. Each time she'd heard it, her
heart had felt as if it had begun to beat directly behind
her tear ducts. Only deep breathing and a rapid change
of subject saved her from tears. Then, just as she

thought she had it all under control, Raleigh Hanlon
would appear in her mind's eye again.

She turned to the woman on her right. "Jade Macleod," she said with forced cheerfulness, "you look
positively sophisticated in black velvet. Of course, ten
years ago you looked sophisticated in jeans and a
sweater." She looked at the attractive blonde on her
other side. "Didn't she, Megan?"

Megan nodded. "Jade looked sophisticated in gym
clothes."

"I do? I did?" Jade asked, as she tore her gaze from
her handsome escort standing across the room from
them.

Relieved to be doing something besides thinking about
Raleigh, Rebecca gave Megan a secret thumbs-up. "Yes
and yes again, Jade. Your assistant can't keep his eyes
off you, either. Every time you're not looking at him,
like right now, he ends up staring at those criss-crossed
straps across your back."

Jade took a speedy glance over her shoulder at the
man surrounded by several drooling women, then turned
back to her friends. She frowned. "Has he been doing
that for long?"

Rebecca and Megan leaned close. "All night," they
both whispered.

The three old classmates turned their eyes again toward the handsome man. He chose that moment to look
their way and give a grin and a big wave. Megan and
Rebecca waved back.

"So, tell us, Jade, what's it like working with *him* and
Congresswoman Bloomfield?"

"Oh, you know Washington," she said, a red blush
staining her fair skin. "Never a dull moment." Looking
decidedly uncomfortable, the pretty redhead attempted

to stave off more questions with one of her own. "Can you believe it? We're back where we all started from, Follett River High. Things never really change, do they?"

"Of course things change. Everything changes," Rebecca said quickly. A little too quickly.

When both women gave her a curious look, Rebecca excused herself and headed for the bathroom. For the next ten minutes, she hid in a stall and tried to figure out what exactly had happened to her in the last month. Outside the stall she heard several old classmates bragging shamelessly about their perfect marriages and pretty babies.

Rebecca drummed her fingers against both arms and tried not to scream. How was she supposed to locate a perspective on her own life with their endless chatter distracting her? While they continued talking about where their lives had taken them after ten years, she glanced downward with a frown. Hers had ended up in the toilet. And no way could she go through with her plans to open a second office in the same town *he* lived in.

Jamming her foot against the commode, she found herself wishing she still smoked. Wishing she still couldn't stand Raleigh Hanlon. And wishing, most of all, that she didn't love him.

"Are you okay in there?" Megan asked from the other side of the door.

"Absolutely fabulous." She dabbed at the corners of her eyes, then opened the door. "Unless you're here to tell me someone found out I've been dropping cherry bombs in the toilets again."

Megan took her by the hand and pulled her back into the gym. "Don't try making a joke out of this. Something happened between you and Raleigh Hanlon, didn't it?''

Sighing heavily, she smoothed the front of her taffeta dress. "I thought I was putting up a pretty good front. Does it show that much?''

"You're holding up quite well, but then you always managed to keep your hurt inside."

Rebecca considered brushing off Megan's compassionate smile. She took a slow, deep breath and ignored the applause coming from the other side of the gym. Probably the old football coach arriving at last. "Ah, Meggie, maybe Jade's right. Maybe we don't change all that much.''

"You know perfectly well that Jade has her mind on something far more important than making sensible small talk." Megan reached out to give Rebecca an affectionate hug. "Hey, of course we've changed."

"Sure," Rebecca said, enduring another hug that was bringing her near to tears. Shaking her head, she pointed to their photo name tags which had been photocopied from their yearbook pictures. "Compared to prom night, just look at us now. Bad hair days and everything considered, we all had dates back then. Now Jade's chosen her very own, very handsome and very interested assistant to escort her. You've refused to date anyone since Andy died. And the man I asked to be my date has, for all intents and purposes, asked me to leave quietly by the back door."

When Megan was finally able to close her mouth, she took Rebecca by an elbow. "What happened between you two?"

"History repeated itself, that's what happened," she said, drawing her hands through a curtain of crepe paper streamers. "I failed his final exam."

Megan nodded slowly. "And will he let you retake it?"

"You mean, even if I wanted to?" she asked with false bravado. "Not likely. He wants to stay as far away from me as he can."

Megan's gaze began jumping furiously between Rebecca's face and something or someone out on the gym floor. The band's music dribbled down to a strangled screech from an acoustic guitar and then ended in a flourish of crashing cymbals.

"What is it?" asked Rebecca, reaching out to her friend. "You look as if you've seen a ghost."

Megan blinked, then settled her gaze on Rebecca's face and shook her head. Rebecca dropped her hands from Megan's shoulders and stood straight up. Instinct told her it was Raleigh. Common sense told her to leave. But it was curiosity, she told herself, and not love that made her stay. Yes, that was it. She didn't love him at all. Never had. Right. Just keep telling yourself that, she thought.

"Hey, Reb, it's Show-No-Mercy Hanlon," someone confirmed with a shout from a cowardly distance. "You'd better run for it."

A ripple of laughter added to the room's growing hum of conversation. Good Lord, did *everyone* in Follett River know about Raleigh and her? She folded her arms in front of her and began tapping the toe of her high-heeled shoe when a single set of footsteps stopped behind her. What was he doing back there? There hadn't been this kind of tension in this room since Mel Frawley's free throw against Barryville.

She narrowed her eyes at Megan, hoping her friend would clue her in.

"Like I said, things have been darn dull around here since you left. But not anymore," Megan whispered before slipping into the curious crowd now circled around them.

"Miss Barnett."

The effect of his voice on her body was truly amazing. He could still stop her dead in her tracks with it, then send shivers up her spine. She closed her eyes. So could his whispers. Especially his whispers.

"Yes, Mr. Hanlon?" she asked, turning slowly to face him as her courage began to fail her. Fine time for that! She was going to survive this moment, even it meant she'd have to leave Follett River and never return. "You wanted something?"

"Mercy, Miss Barnett."

A rumble of fear and a spark of hope filled her chest as he took her hand and drew her out on the dance floor. "What are you doing?"

"Taking a page from your book. You always did love an audience when you were trying to make your point."

The music began with a few soft, sexy notes from a saxophone. He slid his hand around to the small of her back and lifted his other. She looked around the room, then placed her hand in his. Every eye in the place was on them and Raleigh appeared to be loving it.

At first he kept a respectful space between them. Good thing, she thought. Otherwise she'd have bolted from the place, or maybe merely melted. She closed her eyes, fighting the urge to press her cheek against that spot on his shoulder that she knew so well.

"Do you know what I'm thinking?" he asked.

"I have no idea," she said, fixing her gaze to his tie as if it were a keyhole on heaven's door. So, she thought, this is how the beginning of a nervous breakdown feels.

"I'm thinking that we need to go out dancing more."

"I—" She stopped to clear a frog from her throat as she looked at her old classmates forming a thickening circle around them. "What are you doing here?"

"You asked me to come. Remember?"

"And then I told you I was letting you off the hook. I want to know what you're doing."

"Getting smart," he said, keeping their steps tight and to the center of the circle so no one could hear them. "Every teacher worth his salt hopes and waits for the day his student can teach him something. I've been learning from you all month, but today you gave me the big lesson."

She looked up at him through her lashes. His light-hearted smile had settled into a serious expression.

"You were right, Rebecca. I chose to allow Buddy's death to affect my entire life. And although I'll always feel some guilt over the way he died, I've come to realize that I have to let him go and get on with my own life. I wanted to tell you that when I came up to the apartment earlier." He smiled and moved a little closer. "Since you weren't in the mood to listen then, I decided this was the only way it would work."

Any moment now she was going to wake up from this dream and call it a nightmare. His intimate smile reminded her of the way he looked when they were about to make love. He slipped his hand lower on her back causing her to press her hips against his. And she let him, telling herself it was the only way to get through this without making an even bigger spectacle of themselves. Everyone in the room was transfixed by the sight of Reb Barnett and Show-No-Mercy Hanlon dancing. "This public exhibition thing isn't like you, Hanlon," she whispered.

"I can choose to change," he said, pulling her even closer. "Isn't that what you said?"

"Okay, so maybe you are reconsidering some of the things we talked about earlier. You might even be feeling a little bad about how you treated me, but exchanging one kind of guilt for another never works. Knowing you," she said, starting to move out of his arms, "you're going to regret this knee-jerk reaction—"

"What I regret," he said, pulling her back, "is you thinking I was trying to hide you away like a back street mistress. I wasn't. I swear I wasn't." He stopped their dance. "Rebecca, I was just so damned happy being with you that I didn't want to think about sharing you with anyone."

"Is that true?" she asked. Her body began shaking as if someone had sprinkled a bucket of snow over her naked body. "Is it?"

"Hell, yes, that's true," he said, as his voice began to rise. "I love you, Rebecca."

Someone in the crowd let loose with a randy howl. They both looked up and a second later they laughed. "Knock it off back there," Raleigh said in his best teacher voice. The crowd roared their approval as Raleigh wrapped her in his embrace and gave her a kiss that ended any lingering doubt she had about him. Then he brushed her hair off her forehead and whispered, "Now *you* have a choice to make."

"I do?" she asked, still reeling from his kiss. She wiped a smear of lipstick from his mouth then knuckled away a tear from her eye. "And what's that?"

"Would you like for me to take you home first," he said, swaying her in his arms again, "or would you prefer that I ask you to marry me right here?"

She didn't hesitate. "Right here would be fine," she said, looking up into his eyes. "I love you, Raleigh Hanlon."

Epilogue

Pausing outside the window of New Horizon's temporary office on Main Street, Raleigh looked in to see Rebecca tapping a finger impatiently against the fax machine. A slow smile started across her face when she saw him. Ten weeks of marriage and he still couldn't make it through the day without thinking about that smile. And experiencing that now familiar rush of excitement when she turned it on him.

"Delivery from the Chocolate Chip Café," he announced, as he opened the door.

"So Meggie's finally got you to work for her, too."

"Don't knock it, Reb. When I was getting you your caffé latte I heard that the warehouse redevelopment project is moving again. In fact, there's a meeting scheduled for next week at the Maxwell Hotel with the developer. All interested business owners are invited to attend."

"Raleigh, that's wonderful," she said, starting toward him, then stopping when the fax machine signaled an incoming message.

"Waiting for something important?"

"Very important. We're definitely going on our honeymoon the day after your classes end this semester. I'm expecting an itinerary to be coming through anytime now," she said, turning to the fax machine again. "Is it still okay with you that I suggested three weeks touring the Andes instead of Paris?"

He set the paper cups on her desk and began removing the plastic lids. "Well, that's not the most... *conventional* choice for a honeymoon," he said, pretending to reconsider the whole thing. "But then I've thrown that word out of my personal dictionary so..." His glance toward her turned into a fixated stare at her backside. "Are you alone?"

"What, darl—oh, yes," she said, picking up the first paper coming through. "The others are at lunch. By the way, Penny called here this morning. She said as long as she's taking me up on my dare to enroll with me at the college this autumn, she's daring me back to take your history class with her. What do you think?" she asked as the fax continued its humming delivery.

"Hmm," he murmured thoughtfully, as he admired the sleek curves of her body beneath her short, black skirt and sheer, black stockings. Crossing his arms, he leaned against the edge of her desk and studied his wife a while longer. Life didn't get any better than this. "I don't know about that, Rebecca."

"What do you mean?" she asked, looking back over her shoulder as she reached for the second paper sliding into the tray.

He shook his head slowly. "It wouldn't be the same as when you took my history class in high school. There'd be a lot more extra credit assignments involved. I might even have to keep you after class several nights a week."

Reaching out, he curved his hands around her waist. "This time we'd be talking about some major kissing up to the teacher. You did say that we're alone here, right?"

"Raleigh!" she said, turning to playfully swat him with the fax. "Stop tempting me. You have to tell me what you think about this itinerary before you go back to your afternoon classes."

He took one look at the list of exotic names. "This honeymoon isn't going to turn into one of those action-adventure movies, is it?"

"Raleigh, why would you think that? Just because I'm suggesting we spend three weeks in the Andes with nothing but a couple of backpacks?"

He dropped his chin. "That would make most people a little suspicious."

"You're going to love it," she said, handing him the itinerary as she headed for a display rack near the door. "Have a look at these new brochures. There's a lodge—"

He took her handful of travel brochures and pitched them over his shoulder along with the itinerary. "I'll love anywhere you want to go," he said, crooking his index finger then wiggling it to bring her closer. His grin was nonstop.

And that slow smile started across her lips again. "Here?" she asked, glancing at passersby. "In the front window where anyone could see?"

"Yes," he said taking her in his arms. "Am I embarrassing you?"

"I'm...shocked," she said in the most unconvincing way she could.

"Good. I think we should start practicing for the honeymoon," he said, leaning her back in his arms dangerously close to the floor.

She gasped with genuine surprise.

"You didn't think I'd drop you, did you?"

Wrapping her arms around him, she laughed. "The thought never entered my mind."

Without warning he flexed his knees and brought her closer to the floor.

She screamed this time, then burst into laughter.

"Raleigh, don't you dare."

"Beg me," he said, with the insistence of a man who knew he would get what he wanted. In the cradle of his arms, she could only manage another laugh.

"Go on," he said, laughing along with her now. "I want to hear you say it."

"Mercy, Mr. Hanlon."

"Not on your life, Mrs. Hanlon," he said before closing his lips over hers for a spirited kiss.

* * * * *

*Join Susan Connell and Silhouette Desire
for Megan's and Jade's stories in*
THE GIRLS MOST LIKELY TO... *series.*
HOW TO SUCCEED AT LOVE *(Megan's story)*
coming Spring '97.
Jade's story coming soon!

SILHOUETTE® *Desire*

COMING NEXT MONTH

#1045 THE COFFEEPOT INN—Lass Small

January's *Man of the Month*, Bryan Willard, met the most alluring female he'd ever seen—who turned out to be his new boss. He agreed to show inexperienced Lily Trevor the ropes...but he hadn't planned on teaching her about love!

#1046 BACHELOR MOM—Jennifer Greene

The Stanford Sisters

Single mother Gwen Stanford's secret birthday wish was to have a wild romance. But when her handsome neighbor Spense McKenna offered to give her just that, was Gwen *truly* ready to throw caution to the wind and succumb to Spense's seductive charms?

#1047 THE TENDER TRAP—Beverly Barton

One night of uncontrollable passion between old-fashioned Adam Wyatt and independent Blythe Elliott produced a surprise bundle of joy. They married for the sake of the baby, but would these expectant parents find true love?

#1048 THE LONELIEST COWBOY—Pamela Macaluso

Rancher Clint Slade's immediate attraction to devoted single mother Skye Williamson had him thinking that she might be the woman to ease his lonely heart. But would Skye's six-year-old secret destroy their future happiness?

#1049 RESOLVED TO (RE) MARRY—Carole Buck

Holiday Honeymoons

After eleven years, ex-spouses Lucy Falco and Christopher Banks were thrown together by chance on New Year's Eve. It didn't take long before they discovered how steamy their passion still was....

#1050 ON WINGS OF LOVE—Ashley Summers

Katy Lawrence liked to play it safe, while pilot Thomas Logan preferred to take risks. Could Thomas help Katy conquer her fears and persuade her to gamble on love?

FAST CASH 4031 DRAW RULES
NO PURCHASE OR OBLIGATION NECESSARY

Fifty prizes of $50 each will be awarded in random drawings to be conducted no later than 3/28/97 from amongst all eligible responses to this prize offer received as of 2/14/97. To enter, follow directions, affix 1st-class postage and mail OR write Fast Cash 4031 on a 3" x 5" card along with your name and address and mail that card to: Harlequin's Fast Cash 4031 Draw, P.O. Box 1395, Buffalo, NY 14240-1395 OR P.O. Box 618, Fort Erie, Ontario L2A 5X3. (Limit: one entry per outer envelope; all entries must be sent via 1st-class mail.) Limit: one prize per household. Odds of winning are determined by the number of eligible responses received. Offer is open only to residents of the U.S. (except Puerto Rico) and Canada and is void wherever prohibited by law. All applicable laws and regulations apply. Any litigation within the province of Quebec respecting the conduct and awarding of a prize in this sweepstakes maybe submitted to the Régie des alcools, des courses et des jeux. In order for a Canadian resident to win a prize, that person will be required to correctly answer a time-limited arithmetical skill-testing question to be administered by mail. Names of winners available after 4/28/97 by sending a self-addressed, stamped envelope to: Fast Cash 4031 Draw Winners, P.O. Box 4200, Blair, NE 68009-4200.

OFFICIAL RULES
MILLION DOLLAR SWEEPSTAKES
NO PURCHASE NECESSARY TO ENTER

1. To enter, follow the directions published. Method of entry may vary. For eligibility, entries must be received no later than March 31, 1998. No liability is assumed for printing errors, lost, late, non-delivered or misdirected entries.

   To determine winners, the sweepstakes numbers assigned to submitted entries will be compared against a list of randomly pre-selected prize winning numbers. In the event all prizes are not claimed via the return of prize winning numbers, random drawings will be held from among all other entries received to award unclaimed prizes.

2. Prize winners will be determined no later than June 30, 1998. Selection of winning numbers and random drawings are under the supervision of D. L. Blair, Inc., an independent judging organization whose decisions are final. Limit: one prize to a family or organization. No substitution will be made for any prize, except as offered. Taxes and duties on all prizes are the sole responsibility of winners. Winners will be notified by mail. Odds of winning are determined by the number of eligible entries distributed and received.

3. Sweepstakes open to residents of the U.S. (except Puerto Rico), Canada and Europe who are 18 years of age or older, except employees and immediate family members of Torstar Corp., D. L. Blair, Inc., their affiliates, subsidiaries, and all other agencies, entities, and persons connected with the use, marketing or conduct of this sweepstakes. All applicable laws and regulations apply. Sweepstakes offer void wherever prohibited by law. Any litigation within the province of Quebec respecting the conduct and awarding of a prize in this sweepstakes must be submitted to the Régie des alcools, des courses et des jeux. In order to win a prize, residents of Canada will be required to correctly answer a time-limited arithmetical skill-testing question to be administered by mail.

4. Winners of major prizes (Grand through Fourth) will be obligated to sign and return an Affidavit of Eligibility and Release of Liability within 30 days of notification. In the event of non-compliance within this time period or if a prize is returned as undeliverable, D. L. Blair, Inc. may at its sole discretion award that prize to an alternate winner. By acceptance of their prize, winners consent to use of their names, photographs or other likeness for purposes of advertising, trade and promotion on behalf of Torstar Corp., its affiliates and subsidiaries, without further compensation unless prohibited by law. Torstar Corp. and D. L. Blair, Inc., their affiliates and subsidiaries are not responsible for errors in printing of sweepstakes and prizewinning numbers. In the event a duplication of a prizewinning number occurs, a random drawing will be held from among all entries received with that prizewinning number to award that prize.

5. This sweepstakes is presented by Torstar Corp., its subsidiaries and affiliates in conjunction with book, merchandise and/or product offerings. The number of prizes to be awarded and their value are as follows: Grand Prize — $1,000,000 (payable at $33,333.33 a year for 30 years); First Prize — $50,000; Second Prize — $10,000; Third Prize — $5,000; 3 Fourth Prizes — $1,000 each; 10 Fifth Prizes — $250 each; 1,000 Sixth Prizes — $10 each. Values of all prizes are in U.S. currency. Prizes in each level will be presented in different creative executions, including various currencies, vehicles, merchandise and travel. Any presentation of a prize level in a currency other than U.S. currency represents an approximate equivalent to the U.S. currency prize for that level, at that time. Prize winners will have the opportunity of selecting any prize offered for that level; however, the actual non U.S. currency equivalent prize, if offered and selected, shall be awarded at the exchange rate existing at 3:00 P.M. New York time on March 31, 1998. A travel prize option, if offered and selected by winner, must be completed within 12 months of selection and is subject to: traveling companion(s) completing and returning a Release of Liability prior to travel; and hotel and flight accommodations availability. For a current list of all prize options offered within prize levels, send a self-addressed, stamped envelope (WA residents need not affix postage) to: MILLION DOLLAR SWEEPSTAKES Prize Options, P.O. Box 4456, Blair, NE 68009-4456, USA.

6. For a list of prize winners (available after July 31, 1998) send a separate, stamped, self-addressed envelope to: MILLION DOLLAR SWEEPSTAKES Winners, P.O. Box 4459, Blair, NE 68009-4459, USA.

EXTRA BONUS PRIZE DRAWING
NO PURCHASE OR OBLIGATION NECESSARY TO ENTER

7. The Extra Bonus Prize will be awarded in a random drawing to be conducted no later than 5/30/98 from among all entries received. To qualify, entries must be received by 3/31/98 and comply with published directions. Prize ($50,000) is valued in U.S. currency. Prize will be presented in different creative expressions, including various currencies, vehicles, merchandise and travel. Any presentation in a currency other than U.S. currency represents an approximate equivalent to the U.S. currency value at that time. Prize winner will have the opportunity of selecting any prize offered in any presentation of the Extra Bonus Prize Drawing; however, the actual non U.S. currency equivalent prize, if offered and selected by winner, shall be awarded at the exchange rate existing at 3:00 P.M. New York time on March 31, 1998. For a current list of prize options offered, send a self-addressed, stamped envelope (WA residents need not affix postage) to: Extra Bonus Prize Options, P.O. Box 4462, Blair, NE 68009-4462, USA. All eligibility requirements and restrictions of the MILLION DOLLAR SWEEPSTAKES apply. Odds of winning are dependent upon number of eligible entries received. No substitution for prize except as offered. For the name of winner (available after 7/31/98), send a self-addressed, stamped envelope to: Extra Bonus Prize Winner, P.O. Box 4463, Blair, NE 68009-4463, USA.

SWP-S12ZD2

As seen on TV!
Free Gift Offer

With a Free Gift proof-of-purchase from any Silhouette® book,
you can receive a beautiful cubic zirconia pendant.

This gorgeous marquise-shaped stone is a genuine cubic
zirconia—accented by an 18" gold tone necklace.
(Approximate retail value $19.95)

Send for yours today...
compliments of *Silhouette*®

To receive your free gift, a cubic zirconia pendant, send us one original proof-of-purchase, photocopies not accepted, from the back of any Silhouette Romance™, Silhouette Desire®, Silhouette Special Edition®, Silhouette Intimate Moments® or Silhouette Yours Truly™ title available in August, September, October, November and December at your favorite retail outlet, together with the Free Gift Certificate, plus a check or money order for $1.65 U.S./$2.15 CAN. (do not send cash) to cover postage and handling, payable to Silhouette Free Gift Offer. We will send you the specified gift. Allow 6 to 8 weeks for delivery. Offer good until December 31, 1996 or while quantities last. Offer valid in the U.S. and Canada only.

Free Gift Certificate

Name: _____

Address: _____

City: _____ State/Province: _____ Zip/Postal Code: _____

Mail this certificate, one proof-of-purchase and a check or money order for postage and handling to: SILHOUETTE FREE GIFT OFFER 1996. In the U.S.: 3010 Walden Avenue, P.O. Box 9077, Buffalo NY 14269-9077. In Canada: P.O. Box 613, Fort Erie, Ontario L2Z 5X3.

FREE GIFT OFFER
084-KMD

ONE PROOF-OF-PURCHASE

To collect your fabulous FREE GIFT, a cubic zirconia pendant, you must include this original proof-of-purchase for each gift with the properly completed Free Gift Certificate.

084-KMD-R

You're About to Become a

Privileged Woman

Reap the rewards of fabulous free gifts and benefits with proofs-of-purchase from Silhouette and Harlequin books

Pages & Privileges™

It's our way of thanking you for buying our books at your favorite retail stores.

PROOF OF PURCHASE
SD-PP20

Offer expires March 31, 1997

Harlequin and Silhouette— the most privileged readers in the world!

For more information about Harlequin and Silhouette's PAGES & PRIVILEGES program call the Pages & Privileges Benefits Desk: 1-503-794-2499

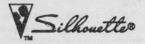

Silhouette®

SD-PP20